Augustin Daly, Gustav von Moser

An Arabian Night in the Nineteenth Century

A comedy in four acts

Augustin Daly, Gustav von Moser

An Arabian Night in the Nineteenth Century
A comedy in four acts

ISBN/EAN: 9783744795821

Printed in Europe, USA, Canada, Australia, Japan

Cover: Foto ©Andreas Hilbeck / pixelio.de

More available books at **www.hansebooks.com**

A N
ARABIAN NIGHT

IN THE

NINETEENTH CENTURY.

A COMEDY IN FOUR ACTS, FROM THE GERMAN OF VON MOSER.

BY

AUGUSTIN DALY.

AS ACTED AT DALY'S THEATRE FOR THE FIRST TIME,
NOVEMBER 29TH, 1879.

NEW YORK:
PRINTED AS MANUSCRIPT ONLY, FOR THE AUTHOR.
1884.

DRAMATIS PERSONÆ AND ORIGINAL CAST.

MR. ALEXANDER SPINKLE, retired broker and ex-Caliph;
a devoted young husband, with a fatal passion for the
ARABIAN NIGHTS . . . . MR. JOHN DREW
HERBERT RUMBRENT, artist and enthusiast, whose pursuit
of the ideal results in his successfully overtaking her,
MR. HARRY LACY
UNCLE MAJOR, a dear old soul to confide in, MR. WILLIAM DAVIDGE
LAFAYETTE MOODLE, not such a fool as he looks for in the
matrimonial market, ... MR. GEORGE PARKES
"SIGNOR" HERCULES BERROWN, Premier Cannon Ball
Tosser, and First Heavy Weight in Boom's Greatest
Show on the Planet . . . . MR. CHARLES LECLERQ
JOHN, Butler at Spinkle's, with a talent for nagging the old
lady, ... MR. FRANK BENNETT
PETER, Waiter at Mrs. Portley's Summer Hotel on the Boule-
vard . . . . MR. HUNTING
MRS. LOUISE SPINKLE, a model wife, i. e., she Believes
everything He tells Her, ... MISS MARGARET LANNER
MISS KATE SPINKLE, an American girl brought up abroad,
and astonished at the ways at home, ... MISS ADA REHAN
MRS. WEEBLES, who being Mr. Spinkle's Mother-in-Law, is
not partial to his Romance, ... MRS. CHARLES POOLE
ROSA MAYBLOOM, a young lady transformed by the Genii of
Haroun al Raschid into what she is not;—but always
captivating Whatever she is. With a fleeting vision of
the "Corsair's Bride," and a brief revelation of the
"Great Indian Act," . . . . MISS CATHERINE LEWIS
MRS. PORTLEY, Keeper of a Summer Hotel on the Boule-
vard, ... MISS SYDNEY NELSON
SUSAN, Chambermaid at Spinkle's, ... MISS GEORGINE FLAGG

INCIDENTAL

To THE FIRST ACT.—Haroun al Raschid, in the privacy of home, reveals an adventure *not* to be found in the Arabian Nights. He's in for it, and in trying to get out opens up a series of hairbreadth escapes of the most thrilling character. The Wild Rose of Yucatan is transformed, and the Caliph escapes for one night.

To THE SECOND ACT.—The Caliph is down on his luck, and Mrs. Spinkle undertakes to have an adventure of her own. The American Girl from abroad undertakes straightening affairs. Mrs. Weebles undertakes matchmaking attempts on the Transformed Beauty, and Lafayette undertakes to assist. Great success of every undertaking except that of Keeping a Secret.

To THE THIRD ACT.—The consequences of the Caliph's nocturnal adventure become more appalling. The stony-hearted Sultan sacrifices his Niece to save himself. The opportune arrival of the Cannon Ball Tosser brings a ray of light. The spell is removed and Rosa becomes for the moment, "The Wild Rose of Yucatan; or, the Modoc Girl Pursued, and the Corsair's Bride." (But—for further particulars—see the play.) Grand Departure of the Beautiful Stranger and her faithful Cavalier, and disastrous overturn of Moodle.

To THE FOURTH ACT.—The Cup of Hope is found to be cracked, and the bright anticipations dribble out. Haroun al Raschid is nailed by his Mother-in-Law, who reigns over Bagdad and the Boulevard for a quarter of an hour. Rosa keeps her promise, however, and saving everybody, leads to a conclusion of Universal Happiness.

The entire action transpires within a day and a half. The first, second and fourth acts pass in Spinkle's house on the Western Boulevard. The action of the third act occurs in Mrs. Portley's Summer Hotel, opposite.

ACT I.

SCENE.—*Spinkle's house. Parlors. Doors* C., *also* R. *and* L.; *window,* L. E.; *fireplace,* R. E. *Elegantly furnished throughout.* MUSIC.

SUSAN *discovered dusting vigorously.* JOHN *enters with newspaper.*

John. Mr. Spinkle isn't up yet?

Susan. [*Snappish.*] I don't know.

John. [L., *looking over papers.*] What's the matter with you?

Susan. I shan't stand their nonsense in this house much longer.

John. Has the old woman been at you again?

Susan. [*Pert, ill-natured.*] Yes; from morning till night, she keeps me a-dusting when there ain't a speck of dust to be found with a microscope, let alone with her old specs. Young Missis was a lady, and let a servant do her own work her own way, but Mrs. Weebles watches and pounces on a poor girl like a cat on a mouse.

John. Same with me. She keeps me everlastingly on the go. It's "John run to the post," or "John run to the drug store," or "John run to the dressmaker's." It's run, run, run, as if I was a young greyhound. Oh, she's a-going it, while her daughter is away.

Susan. [*Advancing.*] How master puts up with her, I don't know.

John. He suffers as much as we do. That's some comfort. She puts him through his paces like a colt. [*Bell.*] Who's that, I wonder? [*Bell.*] I bet it's the old tormentor now!

Susan. [*Crossing to* L., *dusting.*] I ain't afraid of her. Let her ring.

John. She evidently daren't discharge us, or she'd have done it long ago; so we can worry her as much as we like. I love to put her in a passion. It's the only luxury my exhausted system can enjoy. I find she abominates whistling, so I generally give her a concert.

Susan. [*Dusting.*] Here she is.

John. [R.] Is she? [*Begins to whistle, as he arranges newspapers on table.*]

MRS. WEEBLES *enters*, R. U. E.

Mrs. Weebles. [*Brusquely.*] Have you lost your ears? Didn't you hear me ring, Susan?

Susan. Ring, ma'am? Lor'! was it you?

Mrs. W. [c., *to John.*] Stop that whistling, sir! How dare you whistle in my presence?

John. [R., *turns.*] It was only the "Turkish Revelee," ma'am.

Mrs. W. Don't let me hear it again.

John. [*Going up.*] No, ma'am. It *is* getting rather played out, as they say.

Mrs. W. [*Aside.*] Impudent monkey! If I dared to discharge him in Louise's absence! [*To Susan.*] Susan, come with me directly. I want you. [*Exits*, R. U. D.]

Susan. Yes, ma'am. [*Exchanges smiles with John, and follows Mrs. W.*, R. U. D.]

John. [*Whistles very loudly.*] That's a parting salute. I'll serenade her every time I pass her door. I'll teach her to wear a poor devil out! [*Goes to door,* L., *knocks and listens.*]

Spinkle. [L. D., *inside.*] Be there directly.

John. [*Stands aside.*] He's up.

SPINKLE *enters*, L. U. D., *crosses to* R.; *carefully dressed.*

Spinkle. Well, John, what is it? [*Coming to* c.]

John. I've put your newspapers on the table as usual, sir. [*Mysteriously.*] But not your letters.

Sp. [*Stage,* R.] Well—and why not the letters as usual?

John. Because, sir—yesterday—entering the room unawares, —I perceived your mother-in-law examining the correspondence very closely—putting on her specs to look at the postmarks and the handwriting. [*Takes letters from his pocket.*]

Sp. [*Snatches letters.*] That's a pretty cool proceeding. [*Crosses to* L.]

John. I knew you'd think so, when I told you about it.

Sp. [*Sits back of table.*] I refer to your officiousness, you donkey.

John. [L. C., *hurt.*] Donkeys can be dumb, sir. They have ears, but they havn't any tongues. P'raps it was as well I *was* a donkey yesterday, when old Missis asked where I went on that errand for you.

Sp. [*Struck.*] Did she? [*Feels his pocket.*] There *are* some things it is not essential for everybody to know, John.

John. Just what I told her, sir, and she chased me out of the room.

Sp. I don't wonder. [*Rises, gives coin.*] Here—you remember, I once told you that speech was silver—

John. And silence was gold. [*Looks at money.*] So it is, sir. [*Puts it in his pocket.*]

Sp. You can go. [*Opens letters, crossing to* R.]

John. That one has been lying in the post office a fortnight, sir; seems to have been misdirected—was a long time getting to you, sir.

Sp. [*Looks at envelope.*] So it was! A letter from abroad, too! And from my brother! [*Begins to read.*]

UNCLE MAJOR *enters,* C. L., *comes down* L. JOHN *takes his hat and cane and exits,* R. D.

Uncle. Ah! there you are. Came to take breakfast and cheer you up in your solitude. [*Shake hands.*]

Sp. [*Reading, not looking up.*] Glad to see you, uncle.

Unc. Something important?

Sp. From brother Ned in Marseilles; you remember, he is in charge of the railway construction there.

Unc. All well I hope?

Sp. [*Surprised on reading.*] He's coming home! and has sent Kate—you know little Kate—his daughter, my niece, and your grand-niece—he is sending her on before him! By Jove! This letter has been detained two weeks. She's *due now!*

Unc. Sent her over before him?

Sp. He had to; it's all explained here—broke up house-keeping, took his passage, shipped his goods, and was kept back himself at the last moment for an indefinite period. [*Gives Uncle the letter, who puts on spectacles and reads.*]

Unc. So, so! [*Gets* R.]

Sp. [*Crossing to* L., *going up to* C.] Where are the papers—if the steamer should be in! [*Turns them inside out hurriedly.*]

Unc. [*Reads.*] "Kate is a real treasure! An American girl with no French improvements; a little independent, like me, and very romantic, like you, my dear old fellow."

Sp. [*Comes down to* L.] I don't see the name. I must inquire at the office.

Unc. [*Folding letter.*] What a surprise for your wife, when she comes home! A great, big niece! She'll be the joy of the house.

Sp. I don't know. My mother-in-law is yet to be heard from. [*Shrinking from him.*]

Unc. [*Quizzically.*] I say, how do you get on with her?

Sp. As if I were living under the supervision of the police.

Unc. Pooh! A fig for her supervision! You've nothing to conceal.

Sp. [*Looks at him meditatively.*] Havn't I? [*Sighs.*]

Unc. What's the matter?

Sp. Do you care to have my confidence?

Unc. If it's "no confidence—no breakfast," fire away; but you know how I hate other people's secrets. [*Sits* L. *of* C. *table.*]

Sp. [*Sits* R. *of* C. table.] I may need your assistance.

Unc. Come to the point.

Sp. You know I went to San Francisco on business two months ago. That was the beginning of the trouble.

Unc. But you took your wife with you.

Sp. Yes, but I had to leave without her, and come back alone. She stayed behind with her sister who was sick. Well—[*Pause.*]

Unc. Well?

Sp. [*Drawing closer.*] Uncle, you have known me a great number of years.

Unc. Ever since you were born, and that is—let me see—

Sp. Never mind the precise date. But you recollect that, left, at an early age, my own master with a handsome fortune, I was always of a romantic and visionary nature. Going about, seeking adventure—

Unc. Particularly at night.

Sp. Doing good! [*Impressively.*]

Unc. I hope so.

Sp. I took as my model my old boyish delight, the wonderful hero of the Arabian Nights—the dear old Sultan Haroun al Raschid. Like him, it was my fancy to go about *silently* studying people and their purposes, *secretly* rescuing the unfortunate when I found them, and rewarding the honest, and *quietly* enjoying the blessings they showered on their unknown benefactor.

Unc. A very sensible, practical, and economical amusement for a New Yorker in the latter half of the nineteenth century, I must say. Ha! Ha!

Sp. Laugh at me; I deserve it. When I married, I gave up all such nonsense, of course.

Unc. Of course.

Sp. A lovely, devoted wife is worth all the fairies of the Arabian Nights rolled into one. [*Half aside.*]

Unc. Louise is a charming creature.

Sp. [*Turning to him.*] And yet, separated from her, as I was recently, the old romantic passion returned.

Unc. Passion for whom?

Sp. [*Impatient.*] For whom? For Haroun al Raschid! The Arabian Nights! For adventure, you know!

Unc. You mean you began your nocturnal prowling again.

Sp. Listen. On the way home from San Francisco, our train stopped at a remote Western station. Amid the motley group on the platform stood a young creature, who seemed to be known, yet friendless. A tear stood in her eye.

Unc. [*Quizzing.*] Excuse me! Wait till I get out my pocket-handkerchief. [*Takes it out*]

Sp. [*Reprovingly.*] Now, uncle, this is a serious matter. [*Takes handkerchief and replaces it in Unc.'s pocket.*] I walked through the throng of staring idiots, straight up to the young girl and proffered my services. I found she was left at this place by a troupe of traveling performers, who had had a bad season and were obliged to beg their way east. This little thing was too haughty to beg. I bought her ticket, and seated her in the car.

Unc. No harm in that.

Sp. [*Very impressively.*] There is no harm in anything concerned with the matter.

Unc. Then what's your trouble?

Sp. My dear uncle, they say that gratitude is a rare virtue. It's as well that it is, for a more inconvenient thing I don't know.

Unc. You mean that you can't get rid of her now?

Sp. Vulgarly speaking, that *is* the difficulty; she calls me the noblest of created beings—her generous preserver—her only real friend.

Unc. You go and see her occasionally, then?

Sp. I've got to go and see her. If I did not, she might possibly come and see me.

Unc. Why not explain the situation to her?

Sp. To a nature so artless and unsophisticated as hers, it is impossible to explain the conventionalities of social life. Besides, she vows that if I cast her off, she will seek the cold oblivion of the grave and leave a letter behind, explaining my heartless cruelty to a sympathizing world.

Unc. My son, this young creature with the tear in her eye is older than she looks. What do you intend to do with her? Or, rather, what do you imagine she intends to do with you? Does she know your name?

Sp. Of course not. When she asked me my name, in order that she might engrave it on her heart and remember it in her prayers, I told her to call me *Haroun al Raschid*.

Unc. What did she say to that?

Sp. She laughed.

Unc. Well, the thing can't go on forever.

Sp. I had hopes of her getting an engagement somewhere out of town.

Unc. An engagement?

Sp. Yes; you recollect I told you she belonged to a traveling company of show people.

Unc. Ah! Is she low comedy or high tragedy?

Sp. [*Rises, comes down.*] Well, hardly. The fact is—she's a bare-back rider.

Unc. [*Rises, bursts out laughing.*] Delicious! Magnificent! Circus, eh? Houp la! I say, this is a nice affair you've got into!

Sp. And yet, I assure you, she is the gentlest, prettiest, most modest, lady-like and refined—

Unc. Bare-back rider.

JOHN *enters*, R. U. D.

John. Mrs. Weebles sends to know if you'll go and look at carpets with her to-day, sir.

Sp. [*Aside.*] Oh, the devil! [*Aloud.*] Say I shall be most happy. [JOHN *exits*, R. U. D. *To Unc.*] It's the sixth time we've spent the afternoon in the carpet stores, trying to make up her mind about a new bedroom Brussels. [*Crosses to* R.]

Unc. [*Gets his hat.*] I wish you joy. If she's at home, I won't stay to breakfast.

Sp. [*Detains him.*] But in regard to the other matter, you must help me to dispose of this young person.

Unc. What's her name, by the way?

Sp. Rosie—sweet name, eh? She's called on the bills the "Wild Rose of Yucatan."

Unc. I say, you've verified the old proverb—no rose without a thorn, eh?

Sp. Will you help me?

Unc. I'll think it over. Be at the club to-night at nine. We'll talk about it.

Sp. I mean to make an end of it, before my wife returns. You must see the girl—invent anything—tell her I've failed in business, or gone into a decline, or had an important call to Behring's Straits—anything to induce her to transfer her affectionate gratitude to a more appreciative person. [*Sees him to door.*] Say you will.

Unc. [*Going up, turns to Sp.*] I'll make up a plan. I say, let me tell the story in confidence to a few friends. Eh? No? It would be a grand success. Houp la! [*Exits*, C. L.]

Sp. [R. C.] Thank goodness, my wife's mother hasn't the faintest clue yet. She has suspicions, owing to the mystery of movement and the precaution I'm compelled to adopt, but, as yet, she has not scented the Wild Rose.

MRS. WEEBLES *enters*, R. U. D., *with a letter.*

Mrs. Weebles. Good morning, Mr. Spinkle! [*He salutes her brow with dutiful respect.*] Your little wife writes that she will stop over at Chicago a few days.
Sp. [*Assumed disappointment.*] A few days! [*Aside, pleased.*] Good!
Mrs. W. [R.] Fond boy! You wish she were coming this very morning.
Sp. [*Absently, quickly,* L.] Oh, no.
Mrs W. [*Severely.*] No! I thought you missed her very much, Mr. Spinkle!
Sp. [*Quickly.*] Oh, yes—I do miss her—in one sense, but in another sense you have made me so comfortable—made our home so charming— [*Putting his hands on her shoulders.*]
Mrs. W. [*Searchingly.*] I was afraid not—you are so seldom in it.
Sp. Business, you know.
Mrs. W. You retired twelve months ago.
Sp. Precisely—and I am still settling up.
Mrs. W. That's all very well as far as the daytime is concerned, but your evenings are spent at the club.
Sp. A perfectly harmless place.
Mrs. W. At least you might be regular at dinner. I waited for you last night till eight.
Sp. How often have I told you *never* to wait for me?
Mrs. W. How was the opera last night?
Sp. [*Absently.*] Eh?
Mrs. W. You said in the morning that you had been invited to the opera and would probably go.
Sp. Oh, yes! It was charming!
Mrs. W. Did you see the whole of it?
Sp. I wouldn't lose a note. [*Hums.*]
Mrs. W. And yet Lafayette says he saw you in a candy store at 9 o'clock buying chocolate caramels.
Sp. [*Aside.*] For the Wild Rose of Yucatan! I'll choke Lafayette when I meet him! [*Aloud.*] You see, when I listen to music I always get dry in the throat.
Mrs. W. But *you* don't sing?
Sp. No, but it makes me nervous to listen to others.
Mrs. W. Take my advice, Mr. Spinkle, stay at home, that will cure your nerves. [*Stage* R.]
Sp. I will, as soon as my wife gets back.
Mrs. W. Ah, then you do miss her very much?
Sp. [*Ardently.*] Very much.

Mrs. W. [*Tartly.*] Notwithstanding all my efforts to make you comfortable. Thank you, Mr. Spinkle!

Sp. [*Irritated.*] What in the name of goodness will satisfy you? When I said I didn't miss her, you froze with maternal indignation, and now when I say I do miss her, you boil over with offended vanity. Have it your own way. I'm done! [*Sits and begins to read newspaper, L. of C. table.*]

Mrs. W. There's no necessity for a display of temper, Mr. Spinkle. [*Aside.*] It's impossible to say ten words to that man without his flying in a passion. [*Sits R. of table and takes newspaper; he turns his back on her, she ditto.*]

Sp. [*Aside.*] It's intolerable. She treats me as if I were her own husband.

Mrs. W. [*Aside.*] When he wanted to marry my daughter, he was sweet enough. Now he's a perfect tiger. That's the way with all of them!

LAFAYETTE *enters, C. L., with light Derby hat and gay umbrella.*

Lafayette. Good morning, aunt. Good morning, Spink, old boy! [*Puts umbrella on front end of piano.*]

Sp. [*Shortly.*] Morning. [*Aside.*] That's another individual I married with my wife.

Mrs. W. [*Sweetly.*] Good morning, Lafayette! I'm so glad you've called.

Laf. [R. C., to *Sp.*] We had a capital time at the club after you left. [*To Mrs. W.*] He comes there so seldom, too. We miss him.

Sp. [*Nervously, coughing.*] Ahem!

Mrs. W. [*Looks up, inquiring.*] He goes there so seldom?

Sp. [*Aside, to Laf.*] Shut up. [*Aloud.*] You'll excuse me. I have particular business to attend to. [*Starts up.*]

Laf. [C.] Don't you go, Cousin Spink! I've got an important communication to make this morning. I want your help. Personal and confidential. Do sit down. [SP. *sits.*] I'm about to get married.

Mrs. W. [*Startled.*] My dear Lafayette—

Sp. I wish you joy. Now you'll know how it is yourself.

Mrs. W. But you never told me a word about it.

Laf. Well, I didn't know it myself till this morning.

Mrs. W. You proposed at daybreak?

Laf. Proposed? Why, I havn't met her yet.

Sp. [*Aside, engaged in newspaper.*] Idiot!

Laf. I heard of her on my way down town. She's a California belle, worth $40,000 a year, travelling east with an aunt;

young, pretty, orphan, none of those abominable fathers-in-law
and mothers-in-law.

Sp. [*Heartily—turns towards him and shakes his hand.*] My
dear fellow, I congratulate you. [*All rise.* Sp. *throws paper on*
L. *table.*]

Mrs. W. Lafayette, what do you mean by your allusions to
abominable mothers-in-law?

Laf. [*Aside.*] Oh Lord! [*Aloud.*] My dear aunt, when
I look about me and see how few mothers-in-law there are like
you, I think it is a matter of congratulation if a fellow has a prospect of none. [*Crosses to* R. *Presses her to resume her seat.*]

Sp. [*To Mrs. W.*] Ingenious way he has of extricating himself. [MRS. W. *tosses head.*]

Laf. [R.] I've got a capital chance of an introduction.
She'll be at the Potlucker's "At Home," this evening. You've
got cards. I want you to go and get in with the aunt—talk me
up, and, at the proper moment—

Mrs. W. [*Decidedly.*] Ask Mr. Spinkle! [*Crosses to* R.]

Sp. [*Back of table,* L.] I should be of no earthly use.

Laf. [C.] But I want you both to come. Now, my dear aunt
—do oblige me—my whole future, you know—everything at
stake!

Mrs. W. If Mr. Spinkle consents to escort me.

Sp. To-night?

Laf. Yes, do consent—that's a lamb.

Sp. No—you see—the fact is—

Mrs. W. [*Shrilly and decidedly.*] I'm sure I seldom ask a
favor—and, as for going out, I don't know when I've put my foot
outside that door. The mother of your wife, of course, has no
right to expect any courtesy or consideration from her daughter's
husband, but if—

Sp. [*Starting up and closing his ears, going to back of writing
table.*] I'll go! I'll go! I'll go! Say no more!

Mrs. W. [*Graciously, smiling on Laf.*] I'll drive to my dressmaker's directly. I know she can fix up my black velvet in half
a day; it will do very well with the damask waist. I will go at
once. May you be happy, my dear Lafayette; may fortune
favor your suit! I'll go directly! [*Exits quickly,* R. U. E.]

Laf. [*Winks and smiles at* Sp.] He! He!

Sp. [L., *rises.*] I'm exceedingly obliged for the pleasant evening you've arranged for me.

Laf. [R., *shakes hands.*] Don't mention it.

Sp. I'll do as much for you. You shall spend the day hunting carpets with her.

Laf. To-day? Impossible!

Sp. Then it's impossible for me to go to the Potlucker's to-night. If I give you my evening, I must have my forenoon. Take your choice.

Laf. [*Sighs.*] Well, if I must, I must. [*Resolute.*] I'll rush her through the carpets.

Sp. [*Stage,* R.] You'll have a delightful time—she's so amusing.

Laf. [*Dubiously.*] Ye—es. [*They go towards door,* R.]

Sp. You must persuade her that you insisted upon taking my place.

Laf. I'm in your power.

Sp. Exactly, and when you are married, you can take it out of somebody else. [*Exeunt,* R. U. D.]

JOHN *enters,* C. L., *showing in* ROSIE.

John. I'll see if the gentleman of the house is at home.

Rosie. [L. H.] You needn't. I know he is. Tell him a lady wishes to see him.

John. What name, please?

Ros. Merely say that a lady has called to see Sultan Haroun al Raschid. [*Crosses to* R.]

John. [*Amazed.*] Haroun al Raschid?

Ros. [*Sharply.*] Did you hear me?

John. Yes, ma'am. Please step in here. [*Opens* L. D.]

Ros. [*Puts parasol on* C. *table.*] Don't keep me waiting. Beware! [*Exits* L. D.]

SPINKLE *re-enters,* R. U. D.

Spinkle. Free for the day. Victoria!

John. Ahem! [*Points to* L. *door, winks and nods mysteriously.*]

Sp. Well, you idiot! What's the matter?

John. Lady in there.

Sp. A lady? Who?

John. [*Mysteriously.*] Haroun al Raschid.

Sp. [*Sits suddenly in chair, dropping his left hand on piano keys.*] What?

John. That's the name she gave me. I put her in there for fear Mrs. Weebles— [*Winks and nods.*]

Sp. [*Rises, indignant air.*] You rascal! What do you mean? [*Drops* R. *hand.*]

John. [*Politely.*] Nothing, sir.

Sp. Get out, you lunatic! The person is very likely a milliner, or something of that sort, come to collect a bill. [*Crosses to* L. MUSIC.]

John. Very likely, sir. The name did have a foreign sound.
Sp. That will do. [JOHN *exits stiffly,* C.] It can't be. She doesn't know my name, nor my address. Of course, she could find out both, but why? [*Goes to* L. U. E. *door, opens it and staggers back.*] It is she!

ROSIE *enters,* L. D..

Rosie. Yes, it is she. You dear, darling, old caliph! [*Rushing to him.*] What? No greeting? No welcome? Arn't you glad to see me? [MUSIC *stops.*]
Sp. [*Looking round nervously.*] How did you find the place? What brought you—
Ros. Are these my thanks for seeking you? I thought you'd be delighted at such an evidence of my gratitude. What a beautiful house you've got! [*Crosses to* R.] What lovely furniture! [*Sits on sofa,* R.] Oh, heavenly!
Sp. [*Aside.*] She's taking a seat. What shall I do?
Ros. How well this would look from the front! [*Crosses.*]
Sp. My dear Miss Rose, I am sorry to disturb you, but this won't do.
Ros. What won't do?
Sp. Your presence here.
Ros. Eh?
Sp. How did you discover my name?
Ros. The name of my benefactor, the only friend I have in this great, big city—I learned it for the sake of having it graven on my heart. [*Rises, takes his arm.*] You called yourself Haroun al Raschid, [*Laughs*] but I know he only exists in the story books.
Sp. [*Aside.*] Ah! She has read the Arabian Nights, too.
Ros. [*Laughs.*] I followed you and saw you come in here. [*Crosses to* R.] I asked a party at the corner who lived in the house with the big garden, and he said "Mr. Spinkle."
Sp. I am both surprised and hurt.
Ros. Oh, don't be afraid. [*Crosses to* L., *turns archly to him.*] I know you're married.
Sp. [*Sits suddenly,* R. *of table.*] You know it?
Ros. Yes. Your wife's travelling out West. She won't be home for a day or two, or an hour or two at least; so we'll have time for a quiet chat. [*Jumps up.*] Oh, there's a piano! What shall I sing you? [*Strikes a few chords.*]
Sp. [*Who has gone* R. *to listen at door, darts forward and closes piano, sits on lid and places his back against it.*] Are you mad? [*Recovering.*] The piano's out of tune—my head aches—I don't feel like music.

Ros. [R.] What a funny man you are. You act as if you wished me in Halifax! It's not so long ago that you called me a poor fluttered dove [Sp. *makes a grimace and tears his hair, glancing timidly at door,* U. R., *all through the scene.*] and vowed to be my friend for ever and aye. I didn't understand it, but it sounded fair.

Sp. [L., *aside.*] My d—d, nonsensical, romantic rubbish! I wish I'd been shot—

Ros. But it seems that your "ever and aye" means about three weeks and a half. That's how long your amiability, goodness, generosity and friendship has lasted. Now, you begin to sheer off. [*Sulkily.*]

Sp. Sheer off!

Ros. [*Warmly.*] But my gratitude and affection are proof against neglect. I have no right to feel offended. Spurn me, if you will! I must be grateful to you still—"for ever and aye." [*Taking his hand and dropping her head on his shoulder.*]

Sp. My child, this is all very noble, but out of place—in this place. It would be appropriate in any other premises. But here I have but one thought, and that is—how soon I can get you to leave. [*Urging her away.*]

Ros. What are you afraid of—your wife won't come.

Sp. But my mother-in-law will. She's in the house now.

Ros. [*Rising.*] Why didn't you say so at once? [*Crosses to* L.] I wouldn't get you into a scrape for the world.

Mrs. Weebles. [*Outside.*] Susan!

Sp. [*Listening.*] There she is now!

Ros. [*Bounding.*] Good gracious! Where's my parasol?

Sp. Quick!

Ros. I can't find it. [*Rushes to door,* R. U. E.]

Sp. Not there!

Ros. Where?

Sp. She's here!

Ros. Ah! [*Darts into room,* L. H.]

LAFAYETTE *enters,* R. U. E.

Sp. [*Not perceiving who it is.*] Good gracious!

Lafayette. Oh, you've not gone yet. I'm glad of it. I've got a favor to ask of you. You see I've got to trot the old lady about all day, and so I lose an opportunity of making a couple of hundred in Wall street. If you would oblige me with—say half that—

Sp. [*Goes to* L.] I'll draw you a check.

Laf. [*Follows him.*] You're ever so good. I'll go with you.

Sp. If you don't stay where you are, I won't bring it. [*Going* L.]

Laf. Oh, no, I'll go with you.

Sp. [*Shoving him away.*] Stay where you are. I'll bring it. [*Exits,* L. D.]

Laf. He seems to be in a very generous mood. I ought to have asked him for five hundred. It's just my luck. But a hundred will carry me through a week's campaign with the California belle. Opera twice—races once—drives three afternoons. I can manage, with economy, on a hundred. At the end of the week I may have prospects to offer as collateral for another raise. [c.]

SPINKLE *re-enters with check.*

Spinkle. Here you are. [L.]

Laf. That makes a little over a thousand I owe you—not so bad for two years.

Sp. Extremely moderate. [*Crosses to* R. *corner.*]

Laf. When I'm married I'll liquidate it all at once. Good-bye, old boy. [*Takes Rose's parasol from* C. *table.*] I'll be back in ten minutes to take my dear old aunty off for a stroll among the Brussels and Axminsters. Bye-bye. [*Exits,* C. L.]

Sp. Now, to get the Wild Rose of Yucatan out before the dragon has finished her toilette. [*Going towards* L. D., *times it so as to get halfway as* MRS. W. *enters.*]

MRS. WEEBLES *enters,* R. U. D., *in walking costume, buttoning her gloves.*

Mrs. Weebles. Is Lafayette gone?

Sp. [*Meeting her and bringing her* C.] He'll be back in ten minutes.

Mrs. W. [*Passing round to* L. *of Sp.*] Then we have time to discuss his prospects.

Sp. Oh, yes. [*Aside.*] I feel very much like discussing his prospects! [*Gently urging her across to* R.]

Mrs. W. [R.] Lafayette is a good fellow—a little wanting in balance, of course, and almost at the end of his resources.

Sp. [*Buttoning his coat.*] Altogether at the end of his resources. [*Crosses to* R.]

Mrs. W. We must help him to a wife.

Sp. [*Nervously glancing at door,* L.] You are right—quite right—but, I say, you are not going out in this dress?

Mrs. W. Why not?

2

Sp. My dear mother, you will catch your death of cold. The weather has changed. Go and put on something else, there's a dear.

Mrs. W. This is my warmest dress.

Sp. Is it? That's the difficulty. You run about—you get overheated in the shops—you come out and get chilled through. Put on something thinner.

Mrs. W. Then I *should* freeze. What are you thinking of? [*Crosses*, R.]

Sp. [*Aside.*] How to get you back into your room! [*Whistling outside, "Fatinitza."*]

Mrs. W. [*Crossing*, L.] Who's that whistling?

Sp. [*Aside.*] The Wild Rose. [*Aloud.*] It must be John.

Mrs. W. Servants whistling through the house! You must stop it. Wait, let me go.

Sp. [*Detains her, gets* L.] Leave him to me—you are too mild with him. I will simply throw him out of the window. That will be equivalent to a discharge.

Mrs. W. [R.] Whistling in a respectable house! I warned him once this morning, but he don't mind *me*.

Sp. I'll teach him to pay you proper respect. Now, my dear mamma, do let me persuade you to change your dress.

Mrs. W. I might put on my Organdie with the purple flower.

Sp. [*Looking over his shoulder, to* L.] The very thing, put on the purple with the Organdie flower.

Mrs. W. I really need a new dress—I haven't actually got a rag fit to wear.

Sp. Why not get what you want while you are out to-day? [*With feeling.*] The mother of my wife must want for nothing.

Mrs. W. [*Rising.*] Oh, Alexander, if you were always as kind and considerate as this!

Sp. Don't mention it.

Mrs. W. I'll go at once and change my dress.

Sp. Do, and don't hurry. [*Accompanies her to door.*]

Mrs. W. You *are* a dear darling! If I had Louise to give over again, you should have her. [*Exits*, R. U. D.]

Sp. Costly but effective strategy! Now, then—[*Goes to* L. *and opens door, calls softly.*] Miss Rose! [*Timidly peeps after Mrs. W.*, R. D.]

ROSIE *enters*, L., *yawning, with a book in her hand.*

Rosie. This is a jolly book. Why can't I finish it now I've begun it?

Sp. [*Coming down*, C.] Take it with you.

Ros. [*Pouts.*] But I want to stay there—curled up in that big chair. [*Indicates room,* L.]

Sp. [L.] If you lose this opportunity of getting away, you'll have to stay curled up all night.

Ros. Oh, I'll go right off. [*Crosses* L., *goes about looking for parasol. He follows nervously.*] Where did I leave my parasol? [L.]

Sp. I'll get you another.

Ros. Mine had a splendid gold handle.

Sp. I'll get you another splendid gold handle.

Ros. [L.] With my name engraved on it?

Sp. [*Getting* R.] Come this way. I'll have your name set in diamonds. Do go.

Ros. [L., *still searching.*] It's miraculous for a parasol to go off like that.

MRS. WEEBLES *enters*, R. U. E., *down* R.

Mrs. Weebles. Susan's gone out, and there's nobody to get out my dress. [*She and* Ros. *perceive each other, and stand down,* R. *and* L., *speechless.* SP., C., *turns, sees them, makes a step forward and stops. Tableau.* MRS. W. *to Ros.*] Whom have I the honor to— [Ros. *looks towards Sp.*]

Sp. [*Comes down.*] Oh, yes— [*After a moment's reflection, nervously trying to make up an explanation.*] Didn't I tell you? [*To Mrs. W.*]

Mrs. W. Tell me what?

Sp. No—I did not. I remember now, it was so unexpected—so sudden! [*Feels in his coat-tail pockets for his handkerchief.*] But that's what always occurs—the unforseen. [*Feels in breast-pocket and touches his brother's letter—a gleam lights up his countenance.*]

Mrs. W. Why, Alexander, what is the matter with you? But you don't introduce the young person.

Sp. [*Draws out the letter, looks at it and smiles.*] My dear Mrs. Weebles, you'll be astonished and delighted when I present to you— [*Takes Ros.'s hand and leads her to Mrs. W.*] My niece, from Marseilles.

Mrs. W. [Ros. *curtseys demurely.*] Your niece from Marseilles!

Sp. Be good enough to read. [*Hands her the letter. She puts up her glasses.*]

Ros. [*Crosses* C., *aside to Sp., as she passes.*] Haroun al Raschid, what are you doing?

Sp. [*Aside.*] It's my mother-in-law. Do as I say, or I am lost.

Ros. I understand. Don't be afraid, I'll get you out of it.

Mrs. W. [*Looking up.*] And you have just arrived this morning?

Ros. [*Curtseys.*] No, ma'am—yesterday.

Mrs. W. Why did you not come to us immediately, my child?

Ros. Oh, I was afraid of putting you to inconvenience. I went directly to a hotel.

Sp. [*Aside.*] What nonsense! [*To Mrs. W.*] And only think, she declares she has now only run in to make us a brief call and must be off directly. Didn't you say so, my dear? [*Aside.*] I've forgotten the name. [*Crosses to* L.]

Mrs. W. [*Looks at letter.*] Kate! Your name is Kate!

Sp. So it is! Kate, Catherine, Kitty. [*Pointedly to* Ros.] Only daughter of my brother Edward, the eminent engineer, who is shortly to follow her. [Ros. *checks off each item of information quietly by a nod of the head.*]

Ros. [*Half laughing.*] Thanks for your kind reception, my dear uncle. I must be going at once. [*Going up,* Sp. *urging her off.*]

Mrs. W. [*Detaining her.*] You shall not stir, my dear child. You must stay and have a chat with me; we must be better acquainted.

Sp. She can come to-morrow. [*Urging Ros. off.*]

Mrs. W. To-morrow! Nonsense! She must be tired, coming all the way up here. [*Rings the bell,* R.] It's strange you never told me to expect her. [*To Sp.*]

Sp. I only received the letter this morning. Ask John.

JOHN *enters,* C.

Mrs. W. Breakfast directly! [JOHN *exits,* C.] Will you have coffee or chocolate? or perhaps you'd prefer a glass of wine.

Ros. M—yes. I'll take a glass of wine first.

Mrs. W. [*Rings.*] Claret, I suppose.

Ros. Ah, the horrid stuff! No! Port or sherry.

Sp. [*Aside.*] Oh, Lord! Wouldn't you like a glass of Apollinaris water? [*Worried.*] I'm afraid she's going to have what she calls a lark at my expense.

JOHN *enters,* C.

Mrs. W. [R.] Port wine, John. [JOHN *exits,* C.] Arn't you afraid it will be too strong for you?

Ros. Bless you, no. The stronger it is, the more I like it.

Sp. [*Stage,* L.] By Jove!

JOHN *enters,* C., *with decanter and glasses and puts them on table,* C. MRS. W. *and* ROS. *sit* R. *and* L. *of table.*

Mrs. W. Now, you shall tell me all about your home.

Sp. [*Aside.*] I must take a hand in. [*Sits at table,* C., *between them, face to audience.*] I beg your pardon, ladies, but this interests me greatly. [*Keeps his hand on the decanter which* ROS. *reaches for.*]

Mrs. W. Fill her glass, Mr. Spinkle.

Sp. Certainly. [*Gives her a drop.*]

Ros. [*To Mrs. W.*] See what a little drop uncle gives me!

Mrs. W. Give the child a mouthful. [SP. *reluctantly gives* ROS. *more.* MRS. W. *passes her the cake and* ROS. *begins to eat and sip.*] How do you find it?

Ros. A 1. [*Eats.*]

Mrs. W. A 1?

Sp. [*Explaining.*] An expression she has probably learned from her father. It is much in vogue with mathematicians and engineers.

Mrs. W. [*To Ros.*] Do you find a great difference between Europe and America?

Sp. Of course she does. There's a difference of 3,000 miles, not to mention the difference in language. [ROS. *holds her glass to* JOHN, *who fills it before Sp. can prevent him; she enjoys the joke.*]

Mrs. W. I suppose you live very elegantly over there?

Ros. M-m-m! You should see us. We kept thirty-one servants, one for every day in the month.

Sp. What do you do in February with the three extra ones?

Mrs. W. That's what we call extravagant.

Ros. I don't care, I always have what I want, regardless of cost. [*Raps with glass on table.*]

Mrs. W. I'm afraid you have been spoiled. [*Presenting cake.*] Have another piece of this?

Ros. Thank you very much, I don't mind having another glass of wine.

Mrs. W. Mr. Spinkle!

Sp. [*Seizing decanter.*] I don't approve of young persons taking wine. Here, John. [*Giving decanter.*]

Ros. [*Holds out her glass.*] Here, John. [JOHN *fills it.*]

Mrs. W. Here, John. [*Holds out her glass, which* JOHN *fills.*]

Sp. Oh, go it! go it! Here, John. [*Holds out his glass, which* JOHN *fills.*]

Mrs. W. I see by the letter you are just ninete en, my dear

Ros. Yes, ma'am.

Mrs. W. You may call me aunt, if you like.

Ros. Yes, aunty.

Mrs. W. I should have taken you for more than nineteen.

Sp. South of France, you know—hot sun—brings them out sooner. Besides, her mother was of Spanish descent.

Ros. From the banks of the Quadalquiver.

Sp. Are you sure of that?

Ros. [*Finishing glass.*] There or thereabouts. [*Coolly rises.*]

Mrs. W. [*Rises, takes* c.] Could we not take the dear child with us this evening?

Sp. Nonsense! She was not invited.

Mrs. W. But the Potluckers would be charmed.

Sp. [R., *winking across at Ros.*] I know Kate would not care for it.

Ros. [L.] No, indeed. I'd much prefer to go to the circus. [L., *attitude.* Sp. *hastily crosses to* c.]

Mrs. W. [R., *to Sp.*] Singular taste.

Sp. [c.] Strange—not at all. The circus is much more fashionable than the opera on the other side. [*Looks at Ros.*] But I see she's resolved to be off.

Ros. [L., *crosses to* c.] Yes—I can't stay any longer.

Mrs. W. John will see you home. Where do you stop, my dear?

Sp. She can take a bob-tail car.

Mrs. W. But she may get lost.

Ros. Oh, I'm too cute a bird to lose myself. Good-bye, uncle, dear. [*Going.*] Good-bye, aunty. [*Exits,* c. l.]

Mrs. W. [*Crosses to* l.] Well, what a little madcap it is! But I like your niece, Mr. Spinkle. She is so extremely natural.

Sp. Extremely.

Mrs. W. No society veneer—no varnish.

Sp. [*Down* R.] You don't find it everywhere.

Mrs. W. [*Keenly.*] Her father must be well off to afford to keep thirty-one servants.

Sp. A millionaire!

Mrs. W. [*Same.*] Any other children?

Sp. Only one.

Mrs. W. She's a most charming girl.

LAFAYETTE *enters,* c. l.

Lafayette. Now, aunt, I'm at your service. I took your parasol by mistake. [*Hands her Rose's.*]

Mrs. W. That's not mine. [*Reads name on handle.*] "Wild

Rose of Yucatan." [*Hands it back to Laf. with a severe look.*]
Why, Lafayette!
   Laf. [*Reads.*] "Wild Rose of Yucatan." [*Hands it to Sp.*]
   Sp. [R., *reads.*] "Wild Rose—" [*Throws it on sofa,* R.]
   Mrs. W. It can't belong to your niece!
   Sp. [R., *gravely.*] I trust not.
   Laf. What niece?
   Mrs. W. [*Takes his arm, smiling and confidentially.*] I'll tell
you all about it. [*Crosses to Sp.*] Good-bye, Alexander, I won't
be long. [*Exits with* LAF., C. L.]
   Sp. Don't! [*Alone*] What a horrible deceit I've practiced!
Fortunately she eluded the inquiries for her address. I must in-
vent some story to account for her sudden departure. The niece
must disappear instantly. I'll write her at once. [*Sits at* L. *table
to write.* MUSIC.]

JOHN enters, C. L., at back.

   John. Are you alone, sir? [*Mysteriously.*]
   Sp. [L., *at writing table.*] Now what is it?
   John. It's not my fault, sir. I don't bring 'em.
   Sp. Bring what?
   John. The young ladies. There's another one at the door.
   Sp. [*Turns up to him.*] Another one?
   John. And just as good-looking as the first.
   Sp. Ask her to come in. [JOHN *exits,* C. L.] I have a pre-
sentiment! [*Jumps up, buttons his coat, crosses stage to* R.]

KITTY *enters, shown in by* JOHN. *She is in travelling costume and
carries a small bag.*

   Kitty. Mr. Spinkle? [*Timidly.*]
   Sp. [R.] Yes.
   Kit. [*Runs and embraces him.*] My dear uncle!
   Sp. [*Aside.*] I thought so.
   John. Master's in luck to-day. Two nieces turned up in one
morning. [MUSIC *stops. Exits,* C. L.]
   Kit. [*Laughs and holds Sp. out at arms' length.*] He doesn't
know me—actually. He doesn't recognize his own niece! Papa
sends you his love a thousand times over. Why, how strange
you look, just as if you didn't know me. But I am—I'm really
and *truly your niece!* [*With a sudden burst of apprehension.*]
But perhaps you didn't get papa's letter!
   Sp. Yes—only an hour ago, though. [*Crosses to* L.]
   Kit. [*Puts bag on table,* R.] Oh! it's all right, then. How

glad I am to find you out all by myself. I came straight to the place. How do I look? Better than when you saw me in short frocks? Am I very big, or very old? How do you *like* me? Tell me that, the first thing.

Sp. [*Embraces her.*] I love you—always loved you. [*Over her shoulder.*] And if you were only three thousand miles away at this moment, I'd adore you.

Kit. [*Kisses him.*] And you look ever so well! So you married since I saw you last? How I long to see dear aunt and have her love me, too. I'll go to her on your arm, all smiles, then run up to hug and kiss her, and enjoy her astonishment at the sudden attack. Let's go at once. [*Tries to drag him.*]

Sp. Impossible, my dear.

Kit. Why?

Sp. In the first place, she is not here, she is out of town.

Kit. Well, then, I must make the most of *you.* Let's sit down and have a long talk. [*Takes off her hat and puts it on* c. table.]

Sp. [*Crosses to* R., *aside.*] The situation is becoming delightful.

Kit. [L. *of* c. table.] How strange you are.

Sp. [R. *of* c. table.] My dear Kate, I must speak plainly. Your arrival has placed me in a very awkward position.

Kit. I am very sorry for that.

Sp. I mean on your account. My wife's absence leaves me, so to speak, without the power to offer you a home here.

Kit. [*Turns away mournfully.*] I understand.

Sp. Everything at sixes and sevens—no order—meals unsettled—I'm half-starved myself—neglected—in fact, quite in despair.

Kit. [*Recovering her brightness.*] Say no more, uncle. Thank goodness I've been brought up to housekeeping. [*Rises.*] I'll straighten things out for you right away, and keep them so till aunt gets home. [*Crossing to* R.]

Sp. [L. C.] No, no, no—there's no necessity for that. I take my meals at my club—or a hotel restaurant. You see everything's upside down at home.

Kit. [R. C., *looks round.*] Everything looks in the very best of order here.

Sp. [L. C.] Oh, yes! This room is all right. They are cleaning house, and have just finished this room. The others are chaos. Then, besides, my wife will bring some of her relatives home with her. You understand, my dear child? I needn't explain further. So I'll have to put you in a boarding-house or something, for a few days.

Kit. [*Stage,* R., *disappointed.*] In a boarding-house! oh, dear! how horrid!

Sp. Only for a few days. After that you'll come and live with us. [*Patting her cheek.*] There's a very pleasant Summer resort opposite. It's just as if you were in our house. [*Goes to window.*] You see, right over there. [*Struck and leaving window hastily.*] Good gracious! My mother-in-law is coming back. [*Aside.*]

Kit. [*Going over to him.*] Well, take me over there.

Sp. You had better look at my library before you go. [*Nervously, door* L.] Step in!

Kit. [*Crossing to window.*] No, I'd better go at once, if I must.

Sp. [*Seizing her as she crosses, and brings her to* L. D.] Yes, yes—you may find a book to amuse—I know you like to read.

Kit. I can come over afterwards.

Sp. No—now. Now's the time. [*Hurries her in and locks door.*] Just in time.

MRS. WEEBLES *enters with paper,* C., *down* R.

Mrs. Weebles. Only think, we met a telegraph boy with this despatch. Louise will be here to-morrow.

Sp. [*Drops in chair,* L., *alarmed.*] My wife! To-morrow! [*Rises.*]

Mrs. W. You don't seem to be greatly delighted!

Sp. [*Forcing.*] Oh, I am, I am very much, frightfully—indeed.

Mrs. W. I must get everything ready at once. [*Picks up bag.*] What's that? Your careless little niece left her satchel.

Sp. [*About to get it.*] I'll take it to her.

Mrs. W. [*Affably.*] No. I'll keep it and frighten her—it will give her a little lesson on order. [*Aside.*] And learn a thing or two. [*Looks at bag. Opens it as she goes out.*] Perhaps. [*Closes it and exits,* R. U. D.]

Sp. Fortunately it *is* my niece's and not the other's! [*Down* L. *and unlocks door.* MUSIC.]

JOHN *enters,* C. L.

John. Shall I bring the young lady's trunk up here, sir?

Sp. [*Savagely.*] No, sir. [*Opens door,* L.]

KITTY *enters*, L.

Kitty. It's lovely. I'll read all the books in it.

Sp. Now we'll be off.

Kit. [*Searching.*] Where's my bag? [*Crosses to* R.]

Sp. Oh, I'll send it over. Somebody took it by mistake. We are so upset here. Any valuables in it?

Kit. Only my diary and brushes.

Sp. It'll turn up when they sweep. Come, my love, come. [*Helps her on with her hat, and awkwardly puts it over her eyes.*]

Kit. You are the most nervous and fidgety uncle that ever was.

Sp. [*Hurrying her off.*] Dyspepsia, my dear. Bad cooking and general neglect. [MRS. W. *calls.*] There!

Kit. Why, you actually pull me along.

Mrs. Weebles. [*In a high voice, outside.*] Susan! Susan!

Sp. [*Terrified.*] Ha! [*Hurries her off,* C.] Quick! [JOHN *shakes his head solemnly.*]

CURTAIN.

———◆◆◆———

ACT II.

SCENE.—*Same as First Act, with the addition of floral decorations for the return of Mrs. Spinkle.* MUSIC.

JOHN *enters,* C., *with a floral piece.* SPINKLE *discovered at* L. *table.*

Spinkle. Put it on the piano. That will do. [JOHN *puts flowers on piano.*] Did you place the other basket of flowers in Mrs. Spinkle's room, John?

John. [R.] Yes, sir.

Sp. Mrs. Weebles gone out, John?

John. Yes, sir; went to the depot, sir.

Sp. Did you hear Mrs. Weebles give any—ahem—directions

about packing her own trunks, preparatory to—ahem—leaving for good, John?

John. I heard her tell Susan to get out her things, because she was going to-morrow, sir.

Sp. [*Aside, relieved.*] Thank goodness! I have only to keep my two nieces out of the house one day longer. [*Crosses to* R., *aloud.*] John!

John. Yes, sir.

Sp. [R.] There are certain confidences I may have to repose in you, John—certain instructions I may give—which it is not necessary I should explain the reason for. You understand?

John. No, sir.

Sp. [*Sharply.*] What?

John. I mean I don't understand, sir, but I shall obey, sir— to the letter.

Sp. [*Relieved.*] Very good. You see, John, a certain lady may call to-day. Nobody must see that person except myself. Now you comprehend?

John. Rely on me, sir. [*Crosses to* R.]

Sp. I shall, John. [*Crosses to* L.] John, you may go.

John. Master knows a man of honor when he sees one. I shall keep the secret like the spoons—locked in my own pantry —I mean my bosom. [*Exits*, R. U. D.]

Sp. [*Cheerfully.*] My wife's mother goes to-morrow. After to-morrow I can cease to be a monster of secrecy and dissimulation, and breathe the air of freedom and innocence. My poor niece! Poor Kitty! I'll go to her at once, and tell her that after to-morrow my house is her home. [*Comes down to window and looks out.*] There she is, at the window of her lodgings! How lovely and amiable she looks! [MUSIC.]

JOHN *enters*, R. U. D.

John. Mr. Spinkle! Mr. Spinkle! They're coming! Mrs. Spinkle is coming! The ladies are here, sir! [*Exits*, C. L.]

Sp. [C.] How glad I am to see my precious little wife once more.

Stage R. JOHN *and* SUSAN *enter with bundles and packages, and exeunt*, L. *Afterwards re-enter*, L., *cross to* C., *and exeunt*, C. L. LOUISE *enters*, C.

Sp. [*Embraces her.*] My darling! Welcome a thousand times. [MUSIC *stops.*]

Louise. [L., *rushes to him and embraces him.*] How glad I am to see you again! A thousand times over and over!

Mrs. Weebles *enters, c. l., and goes directly to* l. *window.*

Mrs. Weebles. Now we'll see where he goes, Louise.

Lou. [*Runs to window,* l.] There he is! There! As sure as I live!

Sp. [*Crosses to Lou.*] Now, what in the name of common sense— [*Goes to window and tries to kiss and embrace Louise again.*]

Mrs. W. [*Pulling him away, sharply.*] Time enought for that nonsense! There he is, Louise! Going into the boarding-house! Actually going into the boarding-house opposite! Well, that beats all!

Sp. [c.] I certainly think my wife might pay a little more attention, at this moment, to her husband, than to the lodger across the street.

Lou. [l., *crosses to him.*] You dear ducky, you are ever so right. [*Kisses him.*] There!

Sp. [*Holds her off, admiringly.*] You are a hundred times prettier than when I saw you last—if that were possible.

Mrs. W. [*Severely.*] You are entirely mistaken, Mr. Spinkle, the poor child is pale with fright.

Sp. Pale with fright? What fright? What has frightened her?

Mrs. W. [l.] You had better ask who has frightened her? The man who has just gone into the house opposite—and who has dogged her to your very door, Mr. Spinkle!

Lou. [*Crosses to him—nestling to him.*] Yes, indeed!

Sp. Sit down, dear, and let me hear about this. [*Puts her on sofa.*]

Lou. [r.] I observed him for the first time day before yesterday, at the hotel in Chicago, where I took breakfast. He sat at the same table and stared me completely out of countenance.

Mrs. W. [l., *seated* l. *of table.*] Do you hear, Mr. Spinkle? Stared her completely out of countenance.

Lou. He beset me with the most embarrassing attentions—handed me the salt, the pepper, the butter, the syrup, a fork, the rolls and two spoons.

Mrs. W. You hear, Mr. Spinkle—the salt, the pepper, the mustard—

Lou. No, ma—the butter.

Mrs. W. It's the same thing, Louise.

Sp. [c.] The butter is a very different thing from the mustard. Continue, my dear.

Lou. He seemed anxious to render himself agreeable to me in every way.

Sp. And finally accosted you?

Lou. No. To do him justice, he never attempted to address a word to me; but when I rose from the table, he rose.

Mrs. W. [*Triumphant, to Sp.*] *He* rose!

Sp. Well, I don't see anything very dreadful in that.

Mrs. W. Just wait and hear what follows.

Lou. From that time he followed me like my shadow.

Mrs. W. [*Half weeping.*] Like her shadow! My poor child!

Sp. Go on—the rest.

Lou. I found him at every turn, gazing at me with intensity. In the street—in the horse cars—in the shops—everywhere.

Mrs. W. Everywhere!

Sp. Nobody can prevent that—go on.

Lou. When I bought my tickets for New York, *he* bought tickets for New York.

Mrs. W. *He* bought tickets!

Sp. He bought tickets because he didn't have a pass, I suppose; and when you got on the train, he followed you into the same car?

Lou. No. To do him justice, he did not attempt to come in the same car with me. But when I arrived at the depot in New York—there he was.

Mrs. W. There *he* was!

Sp. There he naturally would be—since he had bought his ticket. I don't see anything very dreadful, so far.

Mrs. W. Nothing very dreadful, so far! I suppose you would have gone as far as that yourself!

Sp. I would—if I had bought a ticket.

Mrs. W. Nothing extraordinary for a lady to find herself followed by a man for nine hundred and fifty miles! Nothing extraordinary, Mr. Spinkle?

Sp. Well, my love, did he make himself disagreeable in any way?

Lou. Far from it. I dropped my handkerchief at the depot, and he picked it up and handed it to me instantly.

Sp. With his card in it—or a note?

Lou. No, indeed.

Mrs. W. [*Rises.*] A pretty school *you've* been to, Mr. Spinkle! A pretty experience *you* must have had!

Lou. He only followed me from the depot here.

Sp. Well?

Lou. [L.] That's all. [*Goes to window,* L.]

Sp. [*Relieved—crosses to her.*] Is that all? It's not so bad then, after all.

Mrs. W. [R., *rising.*] What more would you have him do? I declare, it's enough to drive me mad!

Sp. [C.] I have nothing to take the man to task for. He was not insolent or impudent.

Lou. [L.] Not at all.

Mrs. W. With your principles, Mr. Spinkle, I shouldn't wonder if you considered the person, on the whole, rather praiseworthy than otherwise.

Sp. [*To Lou.*] At all events, you have nothing more to fear, my love. You are in your own home now, and under my protection. [*Kisses her.*]

Mrs. W. [*Between them, drawing Lou. away.*] Do let the poor child get her things off, and rest after her fatigue, Mr. Spinkle. Come to your room, my love, I have so much to talk about.

Lou. [*Crosses to Sp.—laughingly.*] I won't be long—you are not angry with me?

Sp. Angry, my pet? Never! [*About to kiss her.*]

Mrs. W. [*Draws her off.*] Come, my love. [*Exits with* Lou., R. U. D.]

Sp. [*Alone. Music.*] It was an odd thing, but—pshaw!—I don't wonder a man liked to look at so pretty a woman! And she *is* pretty! Oh, no, I can't blame him for that. [*Crosses to window.*] Kate is there still—she looks this way—she sees me and smiles a good morning! [*Smiles, nods, and kisses his hand to her.*] Good morning, my dear.

MRS. WEEBLES *enters,* R. U. D., *and perceives his signs.*

Mrs. Weebles. What's he doing? Who's he bowing to? [*Aside.*]

Sp. [*Talking to Kate.*] I'll be over soon. [*Nods and smiles.*]

Mrs. W. [*Comes behind him softly and looks.*] A young girl, as I'm a breathing woman!

Sp. [*Nods, kisses his hand, closes window, turns and confronts* Mrs. W., *at first dumbfounded, he recovers.*] Excuse my back, my dear madam.

Mrs. W. [*Music stops, stage* R.] Don't mind me, Mr. Spinkle—pray don't mind me.

Sp. [*Sweetly.*] Have you just come back, mamma dear?

Mrs. W. [*Viciously.*] No, sir. I came in while you were telegraphing across the street.

Sp. Oh! [*Turning away.*]

Mrs. W. The responses to your salutations were exceedingly friendly. May I ask who it is?

Sp. [*Aside.*] I can't bring out another niece. [*Aloud.*] It was a young lady, opposite.

Mrs. W. Oh, I saw as much myself.

Sp. [*Embarrassed and hesitating.*] She looked over with such a smile—such an innocent smile—I greeted her as pleasantly and as innocently. You know how such things happen, yourself.

Mrs. W. Sir! Yes, with young boys—or young, impertinent fellows—but not with married men, Mr. Spinkle.

Sp. You are right—quite right—it was entirely inexcusable. I'll close the curtains, to prevent any recurrence of the circumstance. [*Crosses*, L.]

Mrs. W. [*Aside.*] We'll investigate you, sir—later.

LAFAYETTE *enters*, C. L.

Lafayette. Aunty, good morning—how do you feel after the party? You look as fresh as a daisy.

Sp. [L., *sotte voce, humming.*] "She's a daisy."

Mrs. W. [*Sharply.*] What's that?

Sp. [L.] I merely echo Lafayette's compliment.

Mrs. W. [R.] A very distant echo. [*To Laf.*] And how is our love affair progressing?

Laf. [C.] I have made a decided impression, of course—but I'm afraid it's a waste of time.

Mrs. W. You may not get her?

Laf. I may not want her. You know her forty thousand a year? [*To Sp.*]

Sp. Well.

Laf. Well, it turns out to be her capital. Forty thousand's all she's got in the world. That's not enough for two, you know.

Sp. [L.] Then you propose to pull up?

Laf. Yes—to draw off.

Mrs. W. To back out?

Sp. I say, Lafayette—you have a deal of sentiment in your nature—a warmth as it were—an unselfish, uncalculating, impulsive heart.

Laf. [*Innocently.*] Do you think so? I *did* go it blind at first, to be sure, but I'm so very confiding. [*Crosses* R.] Yes.

Mrs. W. [*Suddenly, to Sp., crossing* C.] By the way, as I was going down in the car, I saw your niece.

Sp. [*Serious*, L.] Oh—you did?

Mrs. W. She looked charming. I stopped the car, got out and spoke to her. She had on the sweetest little hat I ever saw. I made her promise to lunch with us, to-day.

Sp. Lunch with us! Here?

Mrs. W. Where would she lunch with us?

Sp. [*Aside.*] What a diabolical chance! My wife must not see her. I can't pass her off there! Poor Louise! I must get *her* out of the house before the other one comes. What shall I invent? [*Slaps his forehead.*] Let me think! [*Exits,* R. U. D.]

Mrs. W. [*Smiling, with importance to Laf.*] Lafayette, I've been planning some good fortune for *you.*

Laf. [R.] For me?

Mrs. W. You remember my telling you about his niece?

Laf. Just landed—

Mrs. W. There's the match for you. An only daughter—and a fortune simply colossal.

Laf. I say—are you sure of the fortune? These things don't pan out on investigation.

Mrs. W. This is positive—and she's a most lovely creature—a little emancipated in sentiment and ideas, perhaps, but her heart is in the right place.

Laf. Oh—if her heart is in the right place— [*Crosses,* L.] Where is it?—I mean where is she?

Mrs. W. Stay to lunch, she will be here.

Laf. [L.] I guess I'd better dress, eh? You know the first impression is everything

Mrs. W. No, no. You'll do well enough. Besides, I want your assistance in another matter. Promise me to be as secret as the grave.

Laf. It's a very grave secret then?

Mrs. W. [*Mysteriously and catching his arm.*] I surprised Mr. Spinkle communicating with a person at the window opposite.

Laf. What of that?

Mrs. W. [*With a shriek.*] What of that? Oh, I forgot to tell you—it was a young lady.

Laf. Horrible! He! he!

Mrs. W. It is my duty to watch over my daughter's happiness. You must discover who and what this young person is! [LAF. *goes to window and peeps out.*] Is she there?

Laf. [*Hooks up curtains.*] Sitting at the window reading.

Mrs. W. The same. But remember—silence, secrecy and discretion. As soon as you get any information, come to me. [*Exits,* R. U. D.]

Laf. There she is! By Jove, she's pretty! Now she raises her head. She looks this way. [*Twists his moustache.*] Ahem! [*Nods, smiles, etc.*]

SPINKLE *enters* R. *lower door, and sees him.*

Spinkle. What are you doing there?

Laf. [*Turns.*] Oh, nothing—merely—that's a deuced pretty girl over there.

Sp. [*Crosses and closes curtains.*] I'm surprised at you! What will the lady think of us? This is my house, sir, my house—and I must be careful to—to—

Laf. Let nobody look at her but yourself, eh? [*Pokes him.*] I say—who is she?

Sp. [*Crosses to* R.] It is a matter of indifference to me, sir, who she is. Some boarder, some sempstress, or something. I believe you have not seen Mrs. Spinkle yet. Your cousin has just arrived.

Laf. Let's go at once. [*Takes Sp.'s arm.*]

Sp. With pleasure. [*Going.*] I shall not mention this matter to my wife, but don't let it occur again. [*Exeunt,* R. U. D.]

JOHN *enters,* C. L., *showing in* HERBERT.

John. Name, please.

Herbert. [*Looks around.*] I wish to see the gentleman whose wife arrived this morning.

John. *Mr. Spinkle's* wife came home to-day.

Herb. Mr. Spinkle? Well, say to Mr. Spinkle that I entreat a private interview with him on a matter of delicacy and importance.

John. [*Aside.*] Private interview? This must be the person master expected. "Delicacy and importance!" Must be the person!

Herb. [MUSIC.] Well, sir, have you considered me sufficiently?

John. Please step this way, sir. [*Opens door,* L.] In here, sir! [HERB. *enters,* L., *and* JOHN *locks the door.*] I guess he won't see anybody till master gets to him. That's done!

KITTY *enters,* C. L., JOHN *looks at her aghast.*

Kitty. Why, my good man, you seem quite overcome! Is Mr. Spinkle at home? I wish to see him. [MUSIC *stops.*]

John. [*Aside.*] Here's another one! [*Aloud.*] I don't know if you can see him, Miss—

Kit. [*Sits,* R., *takes off hat and cloak.*] Oh, very well, I'll wait; there's no hurry. What's your name?

John. My name is John, Miss.

Kit. Well, John, my *uncle* tells me he is greatly neglected.

John. By me, Miss?

3

Kit. Oh, no, not by you particularly; what servants have you in the house?

John. Servants? There's cook, Miss, and Susan, and the kitchen gal.

Kit. Send them here! or, rather, send Susan up. I'll go to the kitchen myself. [*Rises.*]

John. Yes, Miss. [*Crosses to* c., *aside, going.*] What's all this I wonder? Well, master must look out for himself. I can't lock up no more of 'em. [*Exits,* R. U. D.]

Kit. Poor uncle! He shan't have to take his meals in a restaurant any longer. But we'll begin the reform with one at a time. [*Stage,* L.]

SUSAN *enters,* C. R.

Susan. You wish to see me, marm?

Kit. Are you the chambermaid?

Susan. [R., *independent.*] Yes, ma'am! What do you wish?

Kit. I am Mr. Spinkle's niece, and what I wish is to get this house in order.

Susan. I should think everything was in order *now*.

Kit. My uncle is of a different opinion. As the mistress of the house is not here, things have to take care of themselves. [*Turns away.*]

Susan. I beg your pardon, ma'am! Things do *not* have to take care of themselves, and Mrs. Spinkle *is* here.

Kit. [*Starts, overjoyed.*] My aunt has returned? [*Crosses to* R.]

Susan. Mrs. Spinkle has just got in, ma'am.

Kit. Then we'll give her a little surprise! We'll have the kitchen in apple-pie order directly. Lend me your apron, Susan. You can get another. [*Crosses to* L.]

Susan. [*Catching her spirit.*] Yes, ma'am. [*Unties her apron and ties it on Kit.*] But I say, ma'am, our cook's got an awful temper.

Kit. All cooks have awful tempers, Susan. That's how I get along with them so well. Don't come down while I'm there. I'll go into the cage by myself. Get the linen closet ready for my inspection, Susan; I'll show you a little "old country" housekeeping before you're an hour older. [R.]

Susan. [*Aside.*] Well, she's a queer one, but I bet she understands her bus'ness. [*Exits,* R. U. D.]

Kit. I wonder if the cook is much bigger than I am. [HERBERT *knocks at door,* L.] Who's in there?

Herbert. [*Inside.*] I'm locked in.

Kit. Somebody locked in! Why, the key's in the door. [*Turns it.*]

HERBERT *enters,* L., *puts hat on chair, end of piano.*

Herbert. I beg pardon. The man locked me in by mistake, I suppose, and afterwards forgot me. [*Crosses to* R.]

Kit. [L.] Do you—do you—belong here? [*Aside.*] I wonder if he's a relation.

Herb. Do I belong here? Don't you?

Kit. No, I am a stranger.

Herb. Oh, you've just come, I suppose.

Kit. Yes, I've just come.

Herb. A new chambermaid or something.

Kit. Chambermaid! [*Looks at apron.*] I see. No, I'm not a new chambermaid. I'm a new niece. [*Takes off apron.*]

Herb. [*Quickly.*] Niece of the lady who got home this morning?

Kit. She is 'my aunt.

Herb. How fortunate! Then you will say a good word for me!

Kit. I should be very glad to, but I don't know her.

Herb. [*Crosses to* L.] Don't know your aunt? [*Aside.*] This is a singular family.

Kit [*Indicating seat.*] But I intend to make her acquaintance. May I ask what you wish me to say to her?

Herb. [*Sits* L. *of* C. *table.*] You won't think the less of me, I hope, when I tell you I am an artist. I have composed a great picture—a study of the female beauties of the Arabian Nights—nineteen faces are completed—the twentieth is wanting.

Kit. [R.] Oh, you want somebody to paint the twentieth for you?

Herb. [L.] No. I want somebody to sit for it. I have had an ideal—in my painter's dream world—I saw a face that haunted my visions. One day it came on earth, took shape and stood before me. I saw it in flesh and blood—the ideal! the radiant vision! I said to myself, I must have it—the missing face is there— [*Snaps his fingers.*] my picture is finished.

Kit. [*Rises—forward.*] It must have been a great load off your mind.

Herb. The lady was alone—it was at a hotel—I dared not address her—but I followed her to ascertain where she lived—I said to myself: she must have a husband, or a brother, or a father, or an uncle, or somebody.

Kit. It was a reasonable anticipation.

Herb. I learned at last that she is a Mrs Spinkle, and that there is a Mr. Spinkle. I shall address myself to him.

Kit. That's easily arranged.

Herb. But I am so diffident—so bashful—if you will help me.

Kit. With pleasure.

Herb. [*Looks at her steadfast—hands in pockets, then changes his position.*] Pardon me—you have a beautiful head.

Kit. [*Laughing.*] That's not so bad for such an extremely bashful young man.

Herb. There! Stand just in that position! Don't move! Exquisite! And yet your figure does not match—you should be larger—rounder!

Kit. Pray don't mind me—go on.

Herb. And your hair should be darker.

Kit. [*Smiling.*] Oh, I know my imperfections. I am really a quite insignificant person.

Herb. [*Patronizing.*] By no means—that is, not in my eyes; for you can assist me with your uncle.

Kit. [*Aside.*] Well—such coolness. [*Crosses to* R.]

Herb. [*Fervently, takes her hand.*] May I count on your help? Say yes—do say yes—may I call and get your answer?

Kit. You may if you like—that is—of course—at least—I have no objection.

Herb. [*Following her to* R. *corner and impressively kisses her hands.*] I can never repay you. [*Goes up, takes hat from chair near piano, and pauses.*] Yes—you might be—rounder. [*Exits,* C. L.]

Kit. And he calls himself the diffident and bashful young man! If he got the other nineteen sitters the same way, they must present a collection of very much astonished females. He's driven the cook out of my head. No use in beginning now. [*Crosses to* L.]

LOUISE *enters,* R. U. E., *carrying a small cigar case.*

Louise. I stole away from them to make up my little surprise. How glad he will be to find this gift from me in his desk! [*Sees Kit.*] Who is this?

Kit. [*Aside.*] It must be my aunt. [*Runs to her.*] Dear, good aunt Louise, may I hope to gain a little corner in your kind heart? [*Advances.*]

Lou. [R.] Why, then you are the niece mamma has told me so much about?

Kit. [L.] Yes, I am she.

Lou. [*Kisses her.*] Why did they not send you in to me at once?

Kit. I did not know you had arrived.

Lou. I am prepared to love you at first sight, Kate.

Kit. Just think, I was going down into the kitchen to wake up the cook and take her to task for neglecting uncle. He tells a most dismal story of his sufferings during your absence.

Lou. Indeed!

Kit. But now you are back, the sun shines out again.

Lou. [*Both crossing to* R., *arm-in-arm.*] Come to my room. We are all there, and you can begin to settle down with us at once.

Kit. [R.] I must put on something else. I ran over with this dress to engage the servants in single combat. [*Putting on hat.*]

Lou. [Come, there are no strangers—Cousin Lafayette is the only person—

Kit. [*Crossing and up during speech, turns to kiss her.*] Then I *must* fix up a bit for him, of course. I'll be back soon. [*Crosses to* C., *kisses her.*] Oh, I was so fearful you mightn't take to me. I was, indeed.

Lou. [R.] I've taken to you already. Now hurry back.

Kit. In five minutes. [*Exits,* C. L.]

Lou. Now to put this in his desk. [*Approaches desk,* L.]

SPINKLE, LAFAYETTE *and* MRS. WEEBLES *enter,* R. U. D. *She stops as she sees them.*

Lou. There! You found me out!

Sp. Found you out in what, my love?

Lou. [L.] In this.

Sp. A cigar case!

Lou. For you! I bought it in San Francisco myself, and chose it out of a— [*They go up together.*]

Sp. [*Putting his arm round her waist.*] My own darling! [*They converse up stage.*]

Laf. [*Down* C., *with Mrs. W.*] I understand! I drop in as if by accident.

Mrs. W. [R. C.] Just before lunch—and, after a while, I'll manage to leave you alone with the heiress. She's particularly fond of a glass of wine—her French education. I'll send some up. There, be off with you! She'll be here directly!

Laf. Aunt, you are an angel. [*Going.*] Bye-bye, auntie— bye-bye, cousin—bye-bye, Spinkle! Bye-bye everybody! [*Exits,* C.]

Sp. [*Down* C., *arm around Lou.'s waist.*] My darling!

Mrs. W. I suppose you are anxious to see your niece, my love. She'll soon be here.

Sp. [L., *aside.*] And I must get my wife away before she comes.

Lou. [C.] Oh, I have seen her.

Sp. You have—

Mrs. W. [R., *disappointed.*] She was here and went away again? How unfortunate!

Lou. No, she'll be back in a little while.

Mrs. W. How do you like her? [*Sits on sofa,* R., *with Lou.*]

Lou. Very much. She is all nature and innocence.

Mrs. W. A little want of dignity.

Lou. I did not observe that.

Mrs. W. But full of energy.

Lou. Oh, yes. [*To Sp.*] How old is Kate?

Sp. Eh, Kate? Oh, ah! You are quite right. Her name is Kate.

Mrs. W. Louise asks you how old she is.

Sp. [*Sits,* R. C.] Why, you see—time passes very rapidly— with persons at a distance. Originally she was quite small—very. Now she is grown—much. [*Aside, rises.*] I wonder which niece she has seen. I must take her out of this. [*Aloud.*] My darling, I have a little excursion to propose—for an hour.

Lou. Now? [*Rises and crosses to him.* MRS. W. *restrains her.*]

Mrs. W. The child is not recovered from her fatigue yet.

Sp. [*Aside.*] Another expensive but effectual *ruse* must be resorted to. [*To Lou.*] My darling! [*Leading her aside and confidentially.*] I had intended a little surprise for you—in fact I ordered the articles—but, at the last moment I directed Tiffany to keep them until I brought you to make the choice yourself.

Lou. [L. C., *rapturously.*] Something at Tiffany's for me! Not the solitaires I used to long for?

Sp. [*Smiling.*] Sh! Perhaps.

Lou. [*To Mrs. W.*] Oh, I must go directly.

Sp. [L., *aside.*] I wonder if Haroun al Raschid had to take his favorite Sultana to the Arabian Tiffany's, after every nocturnal adventure?

Mrs. W. Isn't there time enough to-morrow?

Lou. No, indeed! We must go to-day, mustn't we, dearest?

Sp. Instantly darlingest! Get your hat on at once.

Lou. Oh, you duck! [*Rushes at him, takes his head between her hands and kisses him.*] Come, mamma! [*Darts off,* R. U. D., *followed by* MRS. W., *sullenly.*]

Sp. [*Touches bell.*] I must write a line to give Rosie when she returns! If it *was* Rosie. [*Takes out pocket-book, tears out leaf and scratches a line.*]

JOHN *enters*, R. U. D., *going* C.

Sp. You rascal, come here! Did I not expressly tell you that that person must see no one but myself?

John. [L.] I locked him in your room, sir.

Sp. Locked him in my room? Him! Whom?

John. The gentleman, sir—then the lady must have let him out.

Sp. What lady, idiot?

John. [*Confidentially.*] One of them as came yesterday, sir.

Sp. Ah! Which of them? Which—that's the point—which?

John. Which, sir? Why the one with the lovely, sweet expression, sir.

Sp. [*Crosses*, R., *aside.*] If I only knew what kind of taste the rascal has! [*Aloud.*] Was it the first one, John, or the last one?

John. [*Winks.*] The last one, sir.

Sp. [*Writing in book, aside.*] Then it was the *real* Kate, after all. Thank goodness my wife met the right niece. [*To John.*] If the other one comes—give her this—quietly—you understand! [*Gives note.*]

John. Yes, sir—trust me. [*Exits*, C. L.]

LOUISE *enters*, R. U. E., *with hat on*.

Louise. Here I am.

Sp. [*Takes hat and cane.*] And here we go.

Lou. We'll take the elevated.

Sp. To get there sooner! Now we're off!

Exeunt, arm-in-arm., C. L., *as* MRS. WEEBLES *enters*, R.

Mrs. Weebles. Never mind, my fine gentleman! You thwart me in every way, but if I get the information I'm after—and that creature across the way turns out to be an old acquaintance—I'll make you dance to my tune as long as you live. [*Down* L. Music.]

JOHN *enters*, C. L.

John. Young lady asking for you, ma'am. Came in a 'ack, just as master and missis turned the corner.

ROSIE *enters,* C. L.

Rosie. Here we are again.

Mrs. W. [*Receives her with open arms and kisses her.*] Ah! My love! Take off your things! We must be company for each other to-day. My son-in-law has just gone out with my daughter. But we will have a good time all by ourselves. Make yourself at home. I have an order to give. John, follow me! [*Exits,* C. R. MUSIC *stops.*]

John. [*Down* R.] Pst! Pst!

Ros. [L.] Well, donkey!

John. From Mr. Spinkle! [*Gives paper.*]

Ros. Very well. [*Puts paper in her pocket. Aside.*] I suppose I ought not to have come! But I couldn't get out of it.

John. [*Nods and winks.*] You are to read it immejitly—immejitly!

Ros. [*Reads.*] "Make your visit as short as possible. Make some excuse to leave at once. Haroun al Raschid."

John. Any answer, miss?

Ros. [*Crosses to* R., *shrugs her shoulders.*] No. Give Mr. Spinkle my best regards, John.

John. All right, miss. [*Going.*]

Meets MRS. WEEBLES, *who enters,* C. R., *with needlework and package of colored worsted.*

Mrs. Weebles. [*In temper.*] Go down stairs directly. Susan will give you my orders. [JOHN *exits,* C.] They don't mind one word I say. [*To Ros., smiling.*] Now, we can settle down comfortably.

Ros. Yes. [*Aside.*] Until I can get a chance to bolt!

Mrs. W. You were walking with some young ladies when I met you this morning. [*Crosses to* R.]

Ros. Some acquaintances I made coming over.

Mrs. W. [*Arranging worsted.*] You must be very careful. Make no friends here without consulting some of us. It takes us old inhabitants to know the right sort of people from the wrong sort of people.

Ros. So it does.

Mrs. W. Now, tell me all about your papa. [*Both sit.*] Is he coming over very soon? I suppose he has a great deal of property, hasn't he, my love?

Ros. Well, you see, auntie— [*Checks herself.*]

Mrs. W. That's right, darling. [*Kisses her.*]

Ros. You see I never spoke to him about his property, but I've understood that he owns—oh—lots upon lots—

Mrs. W. Of what?

Ros. Everything.

Mrs. W. His estate is immense, then?

Ros. Immense.

Mrs. W. [*Taking Kit.'s little satchel out of her work-basket.*] *Apropos!* You forgot your satchel yesterday.

Ros. My satchel?

Mrs. W. Containing your diary. I confess I read a little of it.

Ros. You did?

Mrs. W. It was very indiscreet of me, but I knew there was nothing in it you would object to my seeing.

Ros. Certainly not.

Mrs. W. The sentiments expressed here are charming.

Ros. Are they? I wonder what they are! [*Aside.*]

Mrs. W. Only a little gushing.

Ros. It's because the ship rolled so.

JOHN *enters, c., announcing.*

John. Mr. Lafayette Moodle.

Ros. [*Rising.*] A visitor! I must go!

Mrs. W. [*Rises, crosses to c.*] Only a relation of ours. A very nice young man. You'll see him here pretty often. [*Gets L. of Ros.*]

LAFAYETTE *enters, c. l.*

Lafayette. Dear aunt. [*Pauses as if surprised.*] I thought you were alone.

Mrs. W. [c., *introduces.*] Mr. Lafayette Moodle—Miss Kate Spinkle, my son-in-law's niece.

Laf. [R., *crosses to c.*] I've heard so much of Miss Spinkle, and her adventurous journey across the ocean, alone! Pray, don't let me disturb you, ladies. [*Aside to Mrs. W.*] She'll do.

Mrs. W. [*Aside to Laf.*] And her fortune is immense. She told me all about it. I'll leave you together. [*Aloud.*] I must look after luncheon, my dear. [*Crosses. Aside to Ros.*] There isn't such another young man in the United States. You must like him. [*Kisses her and exits, R. D., but through the ensuing scene she occasionally peeps out at them from R. LAF. follows her to door.*]

Ros. [*Aside.*] I think I've seen something like him before, on the front row of the orchestra. [*Stage L., and back to R.*]

Laf. [*Advancing.*] You'll have to put up with me for a little while. Will that be hard?

Ros. Oh, I rather prefer a young gentleman to an old lady, for company—any time. [*Sits.*]

Laf. [*Crosses to* R., *sits.*] Do you, now? How innocent! Aunt has told me all about you. She says you'll astonish me. You ain't a bit like a young lady.

Ros. [*Starting.*] That's a nice thing to tell me to my face.

Laf. I mean your manners are altogether your own.

Ros. [*Nettled.*] So are yours. There, now.

Laf. She said you were a sunbeam. I find you a whole sun.

Ros. That's something like. If you want to please me, you must talk right along in that style. [*Puts hand on basket.*]

Laf. Delicious frankness! I'm an oddity myself. [*Titters.*] We'll get along splendidly. [*Takes her hand.*] What a little hand.

Ros. Five and three-quarters.

Laf. Alexandre's?

Ros. Anybody's.

Laf. [*Takes up worsted.*] Are you doing that work? I would like to see you work with those little fingers.

Ros. My little fingers don't want to work.

Laf. Let me see you unwind it.

Ros. The colors might come off on my gloves. Gloves cost money.

Laf. Do! Won't you?

Ros. What do you want to set me at this job for? I thought young gentlemen talked in this country.

Laf. So they do—while the young ladies work.

Ros. I don't work. There are cart-horses and there are race-horses.

Laf. Very forcibly put.

Ros. You like a dashing, spirited racer better than an old, heavy hack, don't you?

Laf. But see how easy it is. [*Unwinding worsted.*]

Ros. You don't look much like a racer.

Laf. Do I look like a cart-horse, eh? [*Titters.*]

Ros. [*Puts handkerchief to her mouth, laughing.*] Not with that harness on.

Laf. I say, call me cousin. We are cousins, you know.

Ros. Are we?

Laf. Yes. Do you like the relationship, or is there anything else you'd like better? [*Tenderly.*]

Ros. [*Rises, down* R.] I don't know—what have you got in the house? I'm precious hungry. When will it be lunch time?

Laf. [*Rings bell, rises and crosses to* C.] Right away. [*Aside.*] Auntie's idea is the right one. She's practical. No nonsense about her. [*Getting* C.]

JOHN *enters with waiter, champagne, bottle open, and glasses, and puts them on table,* C., *then stands back to wait.*

Laf. You like the good things of life, don't you?

Ros. Don't I! In the first place, I hate walking; I love to ride. Then I like to sleep late in the morning. [R.]

Laf. So do I.

Ros. And to sit up late at night.

Laf. So do I. He! he!

Ros. I hate bores—and I adore everybody that laughs—jokes and says funny things.

Laf. I'm full of anecdote. I buy all the comic papers and study the jokes.

Ros. In the Winter, I love a big city full of life. In the Summer, I love the country—with plenty of company.

Laf. Oh, how happy a fellow would be with such a wife.

Ros. [*Aside.*] Aha! [*Crosses to* R.] That's the way the wind blows. [JOHN, *at a sign from Laf., pours out glasses.*] Don't it look pretty! There—it'll run over. [*Drinks it off at a swallow.*] Um—m—m! Nice! [*Both seated.*]

Laf. [*Follows her example.*] With our congeniality of sentiment, we would make a capital match—wouldn't we?

Ros. You mean, hitched together—as a team?

Laf. [*Aside.*] She's decidedly fond of hippodromic comparisons. [*Aloud.*] Yes—how would we do in double harness?

Ros. Do? We'd run away and knock things to pieces.

Laf. Delicious. [*Gets closer.*]

Ros. [*Holding glass.*] Just pour me in some more, will you?

Laf. Well, for heaven'sake—I never met such a sympathetic and congenial soul as your's is.

Ros. Ditto to you. [*Chinks glasses.*]

Laf. [*Stealing gradually towards her.*] You could like me, then?

Ros. You'll pass in a crowd.

Laf. With you on my arm? The busy crowd of life.

Ros. [*Stares at him.*] What a goose you are.

Laf. Am I? [*Puts his arm around her waist.*]

Ros. [*Sharply.*] Be quiet! [*In low tone.*] John's looking straight at us!

Laf. John, go down stairs! [JOHN *exits instantly.*] We are alone. Oh, Kate—dearest Kitty! [*Arm around her waist.*]

Ros. [*Aside.*] He means business.

Laf. I never loved a creature I ever met as I do you.

Ros. Sir!

Laf. I mean I never met a creature I loved as I love you. It is not love—it is adoration—it is frenzy.

Ros. It is champagne. [*Rises; crosses to* L.]

Laf. [R.] No, it is the tumultuous passion of a captive heart.

Ros. I must go away.

Laf. Not till you sentence the slave at your feet. See—I kneel for pity. [*Flings himself on his knee—she moves a few steps —but he holds her hand, and travels after her.*] I love you—be mine—say you will be mine.

MRS. WEEBLES *enters, bursting in.*

Mrs. Weebles. My darlings! [R.]

Ros. Oh! [*Escapes and runs to her.*]

JOHN *enters hurriedly.*

John. Master's coming back.

Ros. [*Shrieks.*] Let me get away! [*Darts off,* C., *pauses a moment to laugh at Laf., and disappears.*]

Mrs. W. [*To Laf., who is still on his knees.*] Get up and don't make a display before the servants.

Laf. [*Getting up.*] But where has she gone? It was all right. I was just at the winning post.

Mrs. W. [R.] Did she accept?

Laf. She was just going to.

Mrs. W. I'll take care of the rest. Go to the library and wait for me—Mr. Spinkle is coming.

Laf. Victoria! [*Off,* C. L.]

Mrs. W. [*Sweetly, to John.*] John, not a word of this to Mr. Spinkle! Not a word, John, and I'll remember you. [*Exits,* R. U. E.]

John. All right, mum. [*Aside.*] The old woman's come down at last.

SPINKLE *enters,* C., *breathless.*

Spinkle. I saw Rosie come up in a cab as we left. Put my wife on the train and told her I'd forgotten my pocket-book! Where is she? I must be sure she goes and goes for good. [*Down* R.]

John. [*At back of table.*] She's gone, sir.

Sp. Gone?

John. Slipped into the reception room as you came in, and

darted out the front door as you came up. I heard it slam just now.

Sp. Thank goodness!

John. [*Putting glasses on tray.*] Beg pardon, sir, but the other party came back.

Sp. What other party?

John. The young gentleman, sir—been waiting ten minutes for you.

Sp. Show him up. [JOHN *exits*, C., SP. *looks at watch.*] Who can it be? I must rejoin Louise.

HERBERT *enters*, C. L., *hat in hand.*

Herbert. Mr. Spinkle? [L.]

Sp. [R.] Yes.

Herb. My name is Herbert Rumbrent.

Sp. What can I do for you?

Herb. You are probably not aware of the object of my visit?

Sp. I am not.

Herb. [*Rhapsodically.*] It is impossible for me to explain myself in one word. You will pardon me for preparing you, as it were, in my own way, for the communication I have to make.

Sp. [*Takes out watch.*] Please be as brief as possible. My time is short.

Herb. Will you do me the favor to take a seat?

Sp. Thank you—I prefer to stand.

Herb. Sir—I am a painter.

Sp. Well, sir, we don't need anything in your line, at present, I believe. [*Crosses to* L.]

Herb. [*Hurt.*] You misunderstand me.

Sp. Then—

Herb. [*Enthusiastically.*] Let me speak! Art, Mr. Spinkle, art, in these days of the realistic, contains sufficient of the ideal to save its votaries from the vortex of materialism. We may compare its progress to a mountain journey over rugged barriers and rocky impediments, all to be surmounted, before a ravishing prospect rewards the weary wanderer for his toil.

Sp. My dear sir, is there any prospect of your coming to the point shortly?

Herb. [*Aside.*] A soul of clay!

Sp. I beg pardon—

Herb. I must convince you at the outset, that those things which are above and beyond the experience of mere vulgar existence, have a right to recognition and regard. There are two roads.

Sp. Very good—oblige me by getting into the shortest one at once.

Herb. You catch the metaphor. We shall soon understand one another. Pray sit down.

Sp. I told you before, I don't wish to. This is my house.

Herb. [*With fervor.*] I know that—that's the reason I called—relying on the courtesy of its master. Follow me for one moment into the realms of the ideal—cast off the bonds of conventional inertion and soar to the imaginary.

Sp. [R] My good friend, you have struck the wrong house, or got the wrong number. My name is Spinkle—Alexander Spinkle—a retired stock broker—the *Doctor* is two doors below, and the insane asylum is some blocks above.

Herb. [*Smiling.*] I'm all right here.

Sp. [*Tapping Herb.'s forehead.*] Yes, but the question is—are you all right *there?*

Herb. [*Crossing to* L.] The jest of stolidity. Sir, whatever be the texture of your mind, it has created visions—it has evoked phantasms—

Sp. It has done nothing of the kind.

Herb. [L.] Dreams are the revel of the delighted spirit, freed from the iron shackles of the will.

Sp. I never dream, sir.

Herb. [*Wipes his brow.*] Well, sir, I don't like to say there is anything wrong with you. Heaven forbid!

Sp. Say what you like as long as you say your say out. Come—be short and sweet and to the point.

Herb. We will come to the point, sir.

Sp. Yes, but *when*—when, my good sir? That's the important question for me.

Herb. [*Rhapsodically.*] As soon as I can obtain your assistance in the solution of a problem born of a vision, but the first principles of which you utterly fail to comprehend from want of power to follow me into the profound regions of the ideal.

Sp. [*Calmly but forcibly.*] You mean to say that I am an ass?

Herb. On the contrary—your appearance bespeaks intelligence.

Sp. Quite enough, sir. I have no more time to spare.

Herb. Have I possibly given offence? It was the last thought in my head. Judge for yourself. I come to speak to you of your wife [SP. *starts.*] and begin by offending you. Nonsense! [*Crosses to* R.]

Sp. [*Stops.*] You come to speak to me of my wife?

Herb. [*Turns short on him.*] Your wife, Mr. Spinkle, is

endowed with such beauty as we would behold, could we crystal-
ize the subtle essence of an artist's dream.

Sp. My wife, sir—

Herb. You would not cause that wife a moment's pain—
rather would you make every sacrifice to secure her pride and
happiness?

Sp. I don't understand.

Herb. Your niece has not told you of my coming?

Sp. [*Struck.*] My niece?

Herb. The young lady I just met. [*Turning away,* R.]

Sp. [*Aside.*] This is some rascal who has got hold of the
matter and comes to threaten. Can Rosa be a party to this
plot? I must outface it.

Herb. Your niece—

Sp. I don't know what you refer to. I have *no* niece.

Herb. No niece?

Sp. No niece!

Herb. [*Aside.*] It's an extraordinary family. The niece
don't know her aunt, and the uncle don't know the niece.

Sp. [*Forces Herb.'s hat into his hands.*] Our interview is at
an end.

Herb. Sir! This proceeding— [*Puts hat on table,* C.]

Sp. There is the door, sir. I invite you to view the prospect
outside. [MUSIC.]

Herb. Sir!

Sp. Don't compel me to make your path any more rugged
than it is.

Herb. Very well, sir.

Sp. [*Crossing to* R., *forcing him out.*] No threats, sir.

LOUISE enters, C.

Herb. We shall meet again, sir. [*Turns to go out.*]

Louise. [*Sees Herb. and shrieks.*] 'Tis he!

Sp. 'Tis he? Who?

MRS. WEEBLES enters, R.

Lou. The man that followed me!

Mrs. Weebles. The scoundrel! My lamb!

Herb. Yes! 'Tis he! My ideal!

Sp. Will you get out, sir?

Herb. My dream!

Sp. Shall I kick you out, sir?

Lou. [*Crossing to Sp.*] Oh, Alexander! [*Throws her arms*

around him—he turns to her, R.—*she passes around him as*
MRS. W. *embraces him. He turns her to* R., *and she falls, sitting,*
on sofa. SP. *throws hat at Herb.* LOU., *trying to restrain his*
anger and looking after Herb., pushes him; he falls into Mrs. W.'s
lap.]

Mrs. W. [*Crossing to Sp.*] Let there be no blood shed.
Sp. Oh, go to the devil—and you, sir—
Herb. A most extraordinary family!

CURTAIN.

———————◆◆◆———————

ACT III.

SCENE.—*Garden of Mrs. Portley's Summer Hotel on the Boule-*
vards. MUSIC.

HERBERT *discovered arranging canvass on small table beside him,*
under a tree, R. C.

Herbert. Singular how little offends some people. Who
would have supposed that party across the way could fly into
such a passion. But the greatest wonder is how such an amiable
girl as his niece could have such a bad-tempered uncle.

MRS. PORTLEY *enters,* C., *from house.*

Mrs. Portley. How do you like working out here, Mr. Rum-
brent?
Herb. It is very kind of you to permit me. I get along
famously. Do you know, I felt some nervousness in asking your
permission?
Mrs. P. Nervousness—and why, Mr. Rumbrent?
Herb. [*Artlessly.*] Because you always look so sour, you
know.
Mrs. P. [*Retreating, offended.*] Sour?
Herb. Pardon me. I meant so—so—dignified.

Mrs. P. [*Fanning herself violently.*] My position requires dignity.

Herb. True, and so does your age. Quite natural.

Mrs. P. Upon my word, Mr. Rumbrent, you have a very happy way of putting people at their ease.

Herb. Have I offended you again? I did not mean to. No one would take you for an old woman. You dress so youthful.

Mrs. P. Don't apologize any further, I beg. [*Aside.*] He has the gift of saying the worst things in the most innocent way.

PETER, *a waiter, enters,* C., *with a small register of guests, laughing quietly.*

Peter. Here's the name the tall gentleman has put down.

Mrs. P. The party with the animals?

Peter. [C.] Yes'm. He's the oddest fish I ever saw. [*Leaves book in her hands and goes up.*]

Mrs. P. [*Feels in pockets.*] Left my glasses down stairs. [*Crosses to* C., *to Herb.*] Can you read the name here? It's a new boarder. He looks like a pirate. With the fiercest moustache—and drives a little pony and a small donkey.

Herb. [*Looks at name.*] Evidently a distinguished character. [*Reads.*] "Hercules Smith, Premier Cannon Ball Performer and Strong Man, of P. T. Boom's Greatest Show under the Heavens."

Mrs. P. [*Gives the book to Peter.*] That's a very long name. What does it all mean? [PETER *exits.*]

Herb. Merely a circus performer. [*Having looked about for his box of colors, he now exits for them by the window.*]

Mrs. P. What a disappointment! [*Goes up a step and returns precipitately.*] Sh! Here he is now.

Looks dubiously at HERCULES, *who enters. He has a closely shaven head, but a very long and fierce moustache—short, brown velvet coat and plaid pantaloons.*

Hercules. [L.] Good morning, ma'am! The landlady, I suppose. They said I should find you here. [*Gives hand.*]

Mrs. P. [*Takes hand.*] Yes, sir. [*Aside.*] What a rough hand he's got. It must be the effect of cannon ball tossing.

Her. I have two objects in seeking you, ma'am. In the first place, Alice and John are not comfortably lodged. Alice has a cold in her eye from a hole in the wall, and John has a cramp in his leg from lying in a narrow rack.

4

Mrs. P. Hey? John and Alice! Who may they be?

Her. Alice is the most intelligent pony of her size in America, and John is the most sagacious donkey in the world. They are worth their weight in gold. I secured them for our show, and will take them with me when my other business is accomplished. [*Crosses to* R.]

Mrs. P. Do anything you like to make them comfortable, sir.

Her. Very obliging. [*Takes out tickets and gives her.*] We show under canvass at Manhattanville, on the 15th proximo. Four admissions. Been doing immense business all Spring—hundreds turned away. Dates all filled for the Summer and Fall. Have you ever seen our show?

Mrs. P. No, sir. Do—you—perform?

Her. [*With dignity.*] I believe I am unequalled in my line —in cannon ball tossing.

Mrs. P. [*Hesitating.*] Cannon ball tossing?

Her. Technically so called—but we improve every day. I now lift a horse with my jaw. The young donkey I have just secured will be a feature of my act. I'll ride him round the circle first and carry him out on my shoulders afterwards. Nothing in it to offend the most delicate susceptibility.

Mrs. P. [*Puts tickets in her pocket.*] We'll certainly go.

Her. Now for the other matter. I am in search of a certain person—

Mrs. P. Pray sit down. [*They sit.*]

Her. Just after we had struck an immense business after a very hard season, we met with a great misfortune. Our leading lady, Mad'moiselle Antoinette Berrown, threw us over—gave us the slip—disappeared.

Mrs. P. Dear me!

Her. It paralyzed us. She was the most accomplished balloon and banner jumper in the profession—unequalled in the bare-back act. You should have seen her in "Diana at the Chase"—it was immense! Well—she left. Her excuse was want of proper consideration from the management. You know they have to be sweetened.

Mrs. P. Flattered, I suppose.

Her. Bless you, there are so many fellows turning their heads with nonsense, that they'll throw you over for a look! I told the old man he must sweeten her. He wouldn't, and she's gone to the other shop.

Mrs. P. How unfortunate!

Her. But we are not without resources—if we can get 'em. Last winter, when we had a run of hard luck in the mining circuit, we lost the most promising young woman that ever trod the saw-dust.

Mrs. P. Lost?

Her. The last seen of her was at the railroad station. Our champion contortionist saw her get into the cars with a gentleman. She was unapproachable as a bare-back rider. You should have seen her in her great Indian act: "Modoc Girl pursued by the Pi-utes;" the press endorsed it. Well, as soon as Mad'moiselle Berrown levanted, the old man said to me, go and find the "Wild Rose of Yucatan"—we'll star her and cut Berrown out.

Mrs. P. "The Wild Rose of Yucatan?"

Her. Pretty title, isn't it? It's her *nom der plum, as we say in French.* It makes a magnificent line on the posters.

Mrs. P. Well?

Her. Well? Ah! oh! yes—that brings me to the point. I have been to the dramatic agencies. She has left no address there, but it is confidently reported that she has been seen in this vicinity, and is believed to reside here. I took lodgings with you to be on the spot. Now, have you seen the Wild Rose? Do you know where she is? [*Jumps over back of chair.*]

Mrs. P. [*Rises, frightened.*] My dear sir, I have never heard of her till this moment.

Her. [R.] She was seen to call at a house in the neighborhood.

Mrs. P. Stay—a young lady engaged board here yesterday—but—impossible—what is the name which the—your young person goes by when not on the stage?

Her. [*Searching pockets.*] The governor gave me the title in full—I must have left it in my bag. I'll get it—don't go—I'll get it in a jiffy.

Exits, jumping over several chairs, and knocking against SPIN-KLE, *who enters, hat in hand,* L. U. E. HER. *then exits,* C. R.

Spinkle. [*Rubs his shoulder.*] The fellow is as hard as a post. [*To Mrs. P.*] The landlady, I believe?

Mrs. P. Yes, sir.

Sp. [L.] A young lady took board here yesterday?

Mrs. P. Miss Spinkle—yes, sir—Number three—shall I show you into the parlor?

Sp. Thank you—one moment. I wish to say that you must make her as comfortable as possible—show her every attention—I will be responsible for all expenses. She will stay here a few days, until my wife is able to receive her at my own house.

Mrs. P. [*Who has looked at him suspiciously at first, is now re-assured.*] Oh! You are married.

Sp. Yes, very much. Now, if you will call the young lady to see me—

Mrs. P. Her room is just there. It opens on the porch. I can ask her to step out here. [*Exits,* R. U. *window.*]

Sp. [*Looks round.*] It's a very secluded spot—in the rear. If I can persuade Kitty to keep the house for a few days, until the danger is over! [*Wipes his brow.*] Would any human being imagine the last blow struck at me? Mrs. Weebles, who was to leave to-morrow, has just announced her intention of staying another week! [*Takes out paper.*] And a note from Rosie informs me that she has decided to take up lodgings in the neighborhood, on my mother-in-law's recommendation, [*Crams it back into his pocket.*] while my wife, who has met the real niece, expects a call from her at any moment. I am here to avert it. [*Sits,* R.] If this continues for one week, I will not answer for the consequences.

MRS. PORTLEY *enters,* R. 3 E.

Mrs. P. She will be here in a moment.

Sp. Thanks.

HERCULES *enters,* C. R., *with note-book.*

Hercules. Here you are—the name in full. Miss Rosie Maybloom—last address, Sidesnap's Agency, New York.

Sp. [*Struck.*] Rosie Maybloom!

Mrs. P. [C., *turning to Sp.*] The gentleman is looking for her address. Wants to see her on very important business. [*Exits,* C.]

Sp. [*Rises, quickly.*] You don't say so. Perhaps I can give him the information he requires.

Her. [*Looking doubtfully at him.*] I don't know. It isn't a very uncommon name. The young lady I mean—belongs to the —ahem! Arena! I am Hercules Serrmith, better known as the man with the iron cheek. [*Attitude.*]

Sp. [*Cheerfully.*] We mean the same person. "The Wild Rose of Yucatan." [*Smiles confidentially.*]

Her. By Jove, it's the same! But I say, what line are you in? [*Examines him critically.*] Ah! Ring-master! What show are you with?

Sp. [L.] N-n-no. I'm not exactly a professional—at best only an amateur—and exceedingly anxious to retire from that. But what do you want with the young person?

Her. [R.] To offer her a first-class engagement—starred in the bills—two acts a night, and two hundred a week.

Sp. An engagement! I guessed it! What good luck!

Her. If she says *done*, I take her to Pittsburg with me to-night.

Sp. She will—you shall! [*Aside.*] It's incredible! [*Aloud.*] This very night!

Her. [R.] Ah! What a loss she was! Did you ever see her do the "Modoc Girl pursued by the Pi-utes?" or the "Corsair's Bride?" in which she jumps through 40 hoops backwards?

Sp. Never.

Her. You've lost a treat. But her number—quick! I must see her at once—strike while the iron's hot! The number!

Sp. [*Draws out crumpled note.*] Everything happens for the best. [*Aloud.*] She is actually in the next street. [*Tears off a portion of the note and gives Her.*] There's your direction. You can't miss it.

Her. May all the gods reward thee! [*Crosses to* L., *up.*] I'll put a girdle round about the block in forty seconds. [*Exits with several springs and a vaulting act,* C. R.]

Sp. [L.] I am saved!

KITTY *enters,* R. U. W.

Kitty. Dear uncle! [*Goes to him and presents her forehead to be kissed.*]

Sp. [L.] Ah, my little Katie.

Kit. I suppose you've come for me. Auntie told you, of course, how we met this morning.

Sp. Yes, my love; but I have not come to take you over, my dear; the fact is, my precious, that I came over to say that an unforseen circumstance requires her immediate attention at some little distance, my angel—that, in short, my darling, it will be a few days before she is ready to receive you— [*Stops.*] my sweet—

Kit. [*Disappointed.*] Oh, how unfortunate.

Sp. And there is another matter we are entirely agreed on with regard to you.

Kit. With respect to me?

Sp. Yes—you understand, of course—that you have been put under our charge, and we stand in *loco-parentis*—that is to say, we are to watch over you as a daughter.

Kit. Yes, sir.

Sp. And our first request is, that you should live most retired while away from our roof. Go nowhere; in fact—be seen by no one.

Kit. Oh, uncle! To live like a prisoner!

Sp. It is the etiquette of the country, my dear. Until we formally present you in society, you are to have, as it were, a sort of secluded existence. Read—play—sew—but do not go out, nor sit at the window.

Kit. Not sit at the window? Why not?

Sp. There is so much impertinence, impudence and audacity abroad in this country, that it is really dangerous for a young person to look out at her window; it is, indeed.

Kit. [*Laughing.*] Why, I'm not afraid in the least. I know how to treat impertinence. [*Crosses to* L.] I'll take care of myself.

Sp. [*Suddenly affecting alarm as he looks at her.*] Why, good gracious, my dear!

Kit. [*Alarmed.*] What is it, uncle?

Sp. Look at your face—I mean, let me look at your face. Turn round—not that way. That way! Now the other side. Why, your cheek is swelled up!

Kit. [*Rubs it.*] My cheek is swelled up?

Sp. You must have caught cold—at the window.

Kit. I don't feel any pain. I guess it's nothing very bad.

Sp. Don't treat it so lightly, my dear. In this country—this climate—it is an exceedingly dangerous symptom. You must not stir from the house until I am satisfied that it's entirely cured. Have you a handkerchief to tie your head up?

Kit. I don't want my head tied up.

Sp. I insist upon your complying with my directions. [*She gives handkerchief and he ties up her jaw.*] It is only for a few days or a week at furthest. [*Aside.*] Until my mother-in-law goes away. [*Aloud.*] On no account remove the handkerchief until bedtime, and to-morrow you must substitute a piece of red flannel for it.

Kit. Oh, horrors! Red flannel! [*Crosses to* R.] Is it really so bad, uncle?

Sp. My duty to your father will not suffer me to omit a single precaution for your safety. You feel better already, don't you?

Kit. I'm just beginning to feel very bad. [*Stage,* R.]

Sp. [*Urging her up to window.*] Then you must go into the house at once—and be very particular about the window, my love. Don't go near the window—pull down the shade as soon as you go in your room.

Kit. Yes, uncle.

Sp. [*Taking package from pocket.*] Here's a pound of candy —assorted—I got for you—chew them on the other side of your mouth.

Kit. [*Takes package.*] Yes, sir.

Sp. [*Kisses her forehead.*] Now go, my love, the air is very damp out here. [*Sees her in,* R.] Poor girl! It's a shame to impose on her, but necessity knows no law, and my mother-in-law no mercy.

HERCULES *re-enters, with hat on, as if from street.*

Hercules. There you are yet. How lucky. You can do me the greatest favor. She'll be here right away.

Sp. [R.] Will she go?

Her. Yes, provided her uncle consents. She must see her *uncle* first, and obtain his approval. Of course, it's a pretext— nobody ever heard of her uncle. There is no uncle.

Sp. You are mistaken, sir, *I* am her uncle.

Her. You? You are joking! [*Pokes him.*]

Sp. I shall insist on her going with you. It is my interest to have her go at once.

Her. Oho! Well! Mum's the word—uncle or not! You're on our side, and a devilish good fellow! Have something with me?

Sp. [*Declining.*] Really, I—

Her. I won't hear no. You must. [*Pulls him up stage.*]

Sp. [*Aside.*] It's the only way to get rid of him. [*Aloud.*] Well, have it your own way.

Her. [*Takes his arm.*] We'll drink to the Corsair's Bride.

They are going, when MRS. PORTLEY *enters,* C. R.

Sp. [*To Mrs. P.*] Remember to take good care of the young lady.

Her. [*Crosses to Mrs. P.*] She'll be here directly.

Sp. No—it's another one.

Her. Another one? [*Pokes him.*] Are you uncle to some more? Ha, ha, ha! You an amateur! Why, you're a regular full blown—

Sp. Come along. [*Hurries him off,* L. U. E.]

Mrs. Portley. Rely on me, sir.

HERBERT *re-enters, with palette, rest-stick, brushes, etc.*

Herbert. I say, Mrs. Portley, has my fair young neighbor been out to-day?

Mrs. P. [L.] You seem very anxious about your fair young neighbor, Mr. Rumbrent.

Herb. No harm in that, is there? I told you how I met her at her uncle's.

Mrs. P. [*Looks at his canvas.*] How would you like to paint my portrait? Would it take long?

Herb. [*Working.*] Not as long as a young face.

Mrs. P. [*Down* L., *nettled.*] Indeed!

Herb. No. You see the wrinkles give an expression that is very easily caught.

Mrs. P. I don't think I'll trouble you.

Herb. [*Aside.*] Now, what in the world is the matter with *her?*

KITTY *re-enters.*

Mrs. P. [L., *sees handkerchief.*] Good morning, miss.

Herb. [R., *rises.*] Are you ill?

Kitty. [C.] I've got a swelled face.

Mrs. P. It must have come on very suddenly. Is it the toothache?

Kit. No. I feel quite well.

Mrs. P. Let me see it. [*Removes handkerchief.*] Why, I see nothing! It's all right *now.*

Kit. [*Feels her cheek.*] It feels all right.

Herb. [*Painting.*] I think you look much better without that thing around your head.

Mrs. P. [*Crossing to* C., *jokingly.*] Who consulted you, sir?

Kit. I'm sure I may as well leave it off. I only consented to please uncle.

Mrs. P. Your hair's all spoiled.

Kit. [*Looks at Herb.*] Is it? I can fix that in a moment. [*Runs to* R. U. *window.*]

Mrs. P. [*Confidentially to Herb.*] Did you hear her speak of her uncle?

Herb. [*Looking up.*] Well, what is there strange about that?

Mrs. P. Nothing, except that the gentleman she calls her uncle told me a while ago he had engaged her as governess.

Herb. [*Reflecting.*] And, now I remember, he told me yesterday that he had no niece.

Mrs. P. [*Shaking her head.*] It looks very bad—very bad.

Herb. Who can you trust? [*Irritated.*] Pshaw! Women are all alike. They havn't the slightest regard for the truth. [*Goes to work.*]

Mrs. P. Well, I never! You are the most gallant person I ever met. [*Goes into house,* C. R.]

Herb. [*Pausing.*] And she looked so innocent! A mere

adventuress, I suppose, like so many others. [*Resolutely.*] But she shall not practice her deceptions on *me*. [*Works.*]

KITTY *re-enters.*

Kitty. He's at work, now. How I should like to see what he's painting. Perhaps I could learn something. [HERB. *turns and looks steadily at her.*] Well? Why do you stop?

Herb. [R.] I can't work when anybody is watching me.

Kit. [*Moving away to sofa.*] Oh! Then I won't disturb you any more.

Herb. Thank you.

Kit. Does it interfere with your work if I remain out here?

Herb. I have no right to complain of that. The guests of the house have a right here as well as myself.

Kit. And if I talk? I have read that great painters like to chat while working.

Herb. I am not a great painter! Humph! Do you feel an interest in art?

Kit. Oh, yes, indeed! Especially in painting.

Herb. [*Aside.*] She is trying to wind her artful net about me! [*Aloud, mockingly.*] Perhaps you paint yourself? [*He is always at work.*]

Kit. I draw a little.

Herb. [*Same tone.*] I should really like to see *your* productions!

Kit. [*Rising.*] If you promise to not be very severe with me, I'll show you my sketch book.

Herb. [*Same tone.*] I should be charmed.

Kit. Mind—you have promised. [*Goes into house.*]

Herb. [C., *pauses.*] I wrong her. She is truth itself, or else there is nothing on this earth a man can trust. [*Rises.*] It is impossible to believe that falsehood can dwell in such a heart.

KITTY *re-enters with sketch book.*

Herb. Let me see! [*Takes book.*]

Kitty. [*As they both look over it.*] You won't laugh?

Herb. [*Pausing at a sketch.*] Did you draw that? All alone?

Kit. [R.] Yes. That was done before I had a master.

Herb. [*Studying it.*] It is certainly a study from nature.

Kit. From memory. It is my earliest recollection of the spot where I passed my girlhood. That dumpy little figure there is myself.

Herb. [*Pointing.*] That's a good figure—the laborer in his coarse garb—spade in hand.

Kit. That is my father.

Herb. I beg a thousand pardons—I did not know.

Kit. Why? Work is no shame. I used to work, too.

Herb. [*Crosses to* R., *aside.*] Then she must be poor. [*Aloud.*] Do you know, Miss Kate, that your efforts are far above mediocrity? Honestly, I am quite surprised. [*Turns over more leaves.*]

Kit. [*Tries to take away the book, as he pauses before another page.*] There is nothing more that would interest you.

Herb. [*Retaining book.*] There's another drawing here.

Kit. [*Same business.*] It's a sketch I began this morning.

Herb. [*Same.*] Well, I want to see it.

Kit. Please! [*Puts her hand on it.*] I was merely trying my skill in drawing from memory again, and I commenced with the first thing that came to my mind. [*Removes her hand.*] There, then, what do you think of it? [*Archly.*]

Herb. If I am not greatly mistaken, it is intended for my portrait.

Kit. Do you really recognize it? How glad I am! Then I'll sketch the head of my aunt for you. You wanted that, you know.

Herb. [*Closing book, retaining it, and looking at her.*] Do you wish to know what I think? It's this—with the talent you possess, you are throwing yourself away in taking the position of governess.

Kit. [*Astonished.*] The position of governess!

Herb. Permit me to speak candidly to you. When I met you in the house across the way, you told me the gentleman was your uncle.

Kit. Yes.

Herb. In my subsequent interview with him, he said he had no nieces.

Kit. He said that?

Herb. And a little while ago, the landlady told me that he had informed her you were engaged by him as governess.

Kit. [L., *laughs.*] What an idea! [*Becomes suddenly alarmed.*] But what does it all mean? He forbade me leave the house, or going to the window, and tied up my face, because he said I had a swelled cheek! [*Tearful.*] I don't know what to make of it all.

Herb. [*Gravely.*] I think I can explain.

Kit. Can you?

Herb. Yes—the secret lies in three words: you are poor.

Kit. [*Amazed.*] Poor? Who told you I was poor?

Herb. You forget you showed me the picture of your home,

and the figure of your father! Your uncle, on the other hand,
is rich, and lives in a grand house. You arrive from abroad—
he is forced by common decency to acknowledge you privately—
but, while he seeks for some means of suitably disposing of you,
he intends that you shall neither be seen or heard of. That's all.

Kit. But what if I told you—

Herb. [*Gives back book.*] You needn't tell me anything.
You have a proud and honest heart—did you not say to me,
" Work is no shame." [*Catches her hand.*] I honor you as
much as if you were loaded with riches. Forgive my bluntness,
and let me say that, while on the one hand, I have made the acquaintance of a noble and charming girl—you, on the other hand,
have made a devoted friend, who will serve you to the utmost of
his humble power. Will you trust me ?

Kit. [*Clasps his hand.*] Yes, I will trust you. [MUSIC.]

Herb. I thank you for that. [*Kisses her hand, and exits into
house.*]

Kit. [*Alone.*] I really don't know what he means, nor what
is the matter. He says I'm poor and he's my friend—he has seen
uncle, and talks as if he knew something, or rather everything.
My head goes round and round, and all I seem to understand
clearly, is—that his face and his words convince me that he, at
least, is honest, and that I may confide in his friendship. [*Looks
towards Herb.'s apartments.*] There is his room ! I heard him
sing this morning—and listened.

MRS. PORTLEY *enters,* C. R., *showing in* ROSIE. KIT. *looks at
Ros. and then exits into house.*

Mrs. Portley. The gentleman said he'd be back shortly.
[MUSIC.]

Rosie [*Sits.*] I can wait here, I suppose.

Mrs. P. Certainly—and here's a paper. [*Points to newspaper
on sofa.*]

Ros. [*Crosses,* L., *and sits on sofa.*] Thank you—I don't
want to read. Have you got anything with pictures?

Mrs. P. There's a magazine. [*Aside, going.*] What a respectable young person to stand on a bare-back horse and jump
through balloons ! She looks like a lady! What is the world
coming to ? [*Exits,* C. D. MUSIC *stops.*]

Ros. [*Throws book away.*] And so they want me to come
back, just as I was getting home-sick for it. [*Rises.*] Every
evening as the clock strikes seven, the old longing comes back.
[*Animated.*] The lights! the crowd! the music! the applause!
the bright ring! the neighing horses! the spangles! the glitter!

Then it's my *entrée!* First a hush—then they announce me—then a burst of music and the cheers from a thousand throats—I walk in air! I vault on Dandy's back—and away in a whirl and a tempest!

HERCULES *has entered and overheard—applauds.*

Hercules. Bravo! bravo!

Ros. Hallo! That you? [*Crosses,* R. MUSIC, *tremolo, and very quick.*]

Her. [*Rises.*] I'm here! You'll come! Star you in every town—your own terms—your own maid—your own horses—your own dresses—your own acts—your own circus, in fact, and the governor on his knees begging you to accept!

Ros. I'm almost ready to say yes.

Her. Say it, and come where glory waits! I see you there now! House packed to the top! Audience howling for the Corsair's Bride! There she is! No—not yet—yes—yes—now! [*Takes her hand and runs up stage with her.*] Let 'em go! and in we come! [*They run down.*] Make your curtsey! Now to right, now to the left! Houp la! And away we go. [*She puts out her foot. He puts her, à l'equestrienne, on to sofa,* L., *where she stands an instant at a chord from orchestra, and sings.*]

Rosie's song.

> Hi! Houp-la! Houp-la! Hey!
> Walk up! Walk up this way!
> It is here you may
> See a grand display
> Of Equitation gay.
> Hi! Houp-la!   [*Torpedoes, etc.*]
> This way! Walk up! Walk in!
> All ready to begin. Bang! Bang!
> Stand out of the way,
> That the riders may
> Your kind approval win. Bang! Bang!

[*At end, falls, sitting on sofa.*]

Her. [*Imitating clown.*] Whoa-a-a! I say, master, the young lady rides well, doesn't she? [*à la Ringmaster.*] Yes, sir, the young lady rides very well. [*à la Clown.*] What will the young lady have now, master? [*à la Ringmaster.*] Ask her yourself, Mr. Merryman. [*à la Clown, to Ros.*] What will the dear, delightful, beautiful young lady have now, Miss?

Ros. [*In affected tone.*] The balloons, please.

Her. [*à la Clown, calling off,* R.] Balloons for the young

lady! Now, then, butterfingers! Let me hold the balloon.
[*To orchestra.*] Gentlemen, a little more catgut—and away we
go! [*Takes a child's kite and pretends to hold balloon.* Music.
Ros. *mounts sofa again and pretends to jump through his balloon
—as she sings through second verse of song.* Her. *now walking
in,* c., *and following her motions à la Ringmaster.*]

Ros. [*Sings.*]

Round and round, with a glance and a smile—
Cantering gaily, all hearts to beguile!
When to my feet of a sudden I spring,
What a joyous thrill goes round the ring!
Hi! Houp-la! Here we are again!
Hi! Houp-la! Houp-la! Hey!
Hi! Houp-la! Houp-la! Hey!
This way! Walk up this way!
It is here that you may
See a grand display
Of Equitation gay. Bang! Bang!   [*Torpedoes, etc.*]
This way! Walk up! Walk in!
All ready to begin. Bang! Bang!
Stand out of the way,
That the riders may
Your kind approval win.

At end, Ros. *falls, sitting on sofa, laughing.* Spinkle *has ap-
peared at* L. U. E., *unseen by them.* Her. *strikes attitude.*

Her. So it's all settled! You'll come!
Ros. [*Jumping up.*] Oh, I forgot! [*Stage,* L.]
Her. What is it?
Ros. There's a party to be consulted.
Her. Who is it?
Ros. He's a Turk—Haroun al Raschid—the Caliph of Bag-
dad—that's what he calls himself.
Her. What a precious fool he must be.
Spinkle. [*Advances.*] He is. You've hit it exactly. I'm
much obliged. [*Shakes Her.'s hand.*]
Her. [R.] Oh, it's you, is it? Well, don't mind anything I
say. [*Goes to easel and begins to paint the lady's face, then mous-
tache, eyebrows and spectacles.*]
Sp. I have the interest of this young lady greatly at heart.
Ros. [*Approaching, and archly to him.*] So much so, that
you wish to get rid of me as quickly as possible. Ain't that
so? [*Crosses to* L.]
Sp. How can you think such a thing?

Ros. Oh, I know. I'm in the way—as your *niece!*

Sp. The fact is, that little deception has placed me in the most embarrassing position.

HER. *takes up palette and brush and puts a few touches to the portrait, and turns chair back to* c. *of stage.*

Ros. I only played the part you cast for me—but I understand. The comedy's over—the curtain rung down, and we've come back to real life. So be it. [*To Her., who advances.*] I accept—there's my hand. [*Crosses to* c.]

Sp. [L.] And my blessing with it. Accept *my* congratulations on your engagement.

Ros. [*Buttoning her glove.*] If you should ever need a witness to the character of your mother-in-law, send for me. As for yourself, I will testify that you are the most generous and the most amiable of men. [*Goes up,* c.]

Sp. [*Aside, to Her.*] Be sure you take her away at once—and when you are off for good—as a token, send me back this card. [*Gives card from his card-case.*]

Her. It shall be done, me Lord. [*Crossing up,* L.]

Ros. [*Starting.*] Oh!

Her. and Sp. What?

Ros. [*Advancing,* c.] I forgot! I'm engaged to be married. The young man will die! Where is my Lafayette? Bring me to my Moodle!

Her. Engaged to be married! [*Leaning back in chair, falls over.*]

Sp. To Moodle!

Ros. [c.] He went on his bended knees. Your mother-in-law made the match.

Mrs. Weebles. [*Outside.*] Very good. Much obliged.

Ros. [L.] It is her voice.

Sp. [*Darts to side—returns.*] Good gracious! She is coming here! Miss Rosie—for heaven's sake—hide—here—in this room! [*Goes to Herb.'s door,* R. 2 E.]

Ros. [*Who has followed him.*] But there's a man in there.

Sp. Explain to him when you get inside. In! [*Pushes her in.*]

Her. What's the row, eh?

Sp. Find out what she wants. I'll be within call. [*Exits,* R. 3 E.]

HER. *sits at table and peeps at* MRS. WEEBLES *and* LAFAYETTE, *who enter,* L.

Mrs. Weebles. I saw him! With a young woman! They went in there!

MRS. PORTLEY *follows them in.*

Mrs. Portley. Well, ma'am?

Lafayette. My aunt wished to look at your house. Very pleasantly situated indeed. [*Looks round.*]

Mrs. P. Most happy to show everything.

Laf. We should like to see your rooms.

Mrs. P. I'll get the keys in a moment. [*Exits,* C.]

Mrs. W. If I could only see the creature's face. If I could only just once find out what kind of a person my precious son-in-law is running after. That must be her room. It's just opposite our house.

Laf. [*Aside, to her.*] We'll manage it. [*Aloud.*] You say that room would just suit you? Perhaps we can look at it. [*Advances, but* HER. *bounds before him and obstructs the way— standing on one leg and balancing a chair on his chin.*]

Her. [R.] This room is occupied, sir.

Laf. And who are you, sir?

Her. Principal cannon-ball-tosser and heavy weight. I swing live jackasses around with my teeth, as you'd swing a cat. [LAF. *retires precipitately to* MRS. W.'s *side.*]

Mrs. W. Why don't you go in?

Laf. I'd rather not. He swings live jackasses.

Mrs. W. [*Advances to Her.*] Do you know the lady who occupies that apartment?

Her. I do.

Mrs. W. Who is she? Have you any objection to tell us that?

Her. Not the slightest. She is our *premiere esquestrienne* and principal bare-back rider.

Mrs. W. [*Retreating.*] Bare-back rider! Your arm, Lafayette! Take me away. I shall faint.

Her. [*Advancing, politely.*] If you should need any further information—

Mrs. W. Take me away! [*Exits precipitately with* LAF.]

SPINKLE *re-appearing,* L.

Spinkle. Have they gone?

Her. Yes.

Sp. What did they want?

Her. To see the girl—but no husbands, present or prospective, for the Wild Rose! We've got her back and mean to keep her. I'll take her off the minute they leave the coast clear.

Sp. Then, let us watch for the right time. [*Hurries off,* R. 1 E.]

Her. Houp la! [*Bounds after him,* R. 1 E.]

Kitty. [*Running out and calling after Sp.*] Uncle! Uncle! [*Disappointed.*] He's gone! How oddly he acted! Ran into my room, locked the door and began to peep through the keyhole, then, all of a sudden, darted out, and all without a word! I don't know what to do. Tell Herbert—I mean Mr. Rumbrent —all about it, and ask his advice? [*Goes towards his window, timidly.*] I hear his voice.

HERBERT *appears, looks cautiously out, does not perceive Kit., then hands out* ROSIE.

Herbert. They are all gone. You can come out. Nobody will see you.

Kit. [*Suppressed jealous emotion.*] I beg your pardon.

Rosie. I guess you won't let on about my being in here.

Kit. [*Bitterly.*] The secret is quite safe with me. What do I care? Why should it matter to me that Mr. Rumbrent—and —and—anybody were together in there?

Ros. [*Goes up to her.*] All this means that it *does* matter to you! [*Looks at both.*] I see how it is! [*Aside to her.*] Don't be afraid. I don't even know his name—have only known him five minutes, and, oh! wouldn't have him as a gift! His room smells like a paint shop! There! Thanks, very much. [*To Herb.*] Bye-bye. [*Runs off,* R. 1 E.]

Herb. Good-bye. [*To* KIT., *who begins to smile.*] Well— what do you think?

Kit. [*Sitting.*] I thought you had found your ideal after all.

Herb. Oh, no! I entertained her at the request of your uncle.

Kit. At the request of my uncle?

Herb. That is, I was mixing colors at the window when she tumbled in on me, propelled by your uncle's energetic arm.

Kit. What can it mean? Was she good looking?

Herb. [*Energetically.*] Oh, no! Far from it! She does not resemble you in the least.

Kit. No? [*They are very close together, and he holds her hand and supports her.*] Ah! [*Sighs.*] How uncomfortable all this makes me! [*He starts.*] I mean my uncle's strange behavior.

Herb. Otherwise?

Kit. Oh, if it were not for that, I should be perfectly happy.

Herb. I will seek your uncle and demand an explanation. Have you any brothers?

Kit. No. I am all alone. No one to lean upon! [*Leaning against him.*]

Herb. My heart aches for you. I have no sister; you shall be mine, so look cheerily! Smile! We have nothing to fear. Now, you look radiant! Painters must not lose such opportunities. I'll get my brushes. You'll let me take your picture— won't you?

Kit. I am sorry I can give you nothing more valuable.

Herb. I am content. [*Kisses her hand.*] Wait here! [*Runs in, R. 2 E.*]

Kit. I know what is happening to me. I am falling in love. My heart's in my throat. I'm going to lose it. [*Sits, L. C.*]

LAFAYETTE *re-enters*, C.

Lafayette. There she is, alone! I never talked to a bare-back rider in my life. The brilliancy and dash of a man of the world must be irresistible with 'em! Ahem! [Kit. *starts and turns.*] Don't start, fair lady. Let me present myself, Mr. Lafayette Moodle.

Kit. Have you not made a mistake, sir?

Laf. I believe not. [*Puts his hat on the palette.*]

Kit. I have no recollection of seeing you.

Laf. But I have seen you—exchanging very friendly greetings with a gentleman opposite your window.

Kit. [*Recalling.*] Oh, yes, it was my uncle.

Laf. Your uncle? [*Aside.*] Very clever! She is a ready hand. [*Aloud.*] Exactly! Well, one of the bright rays from your eyes missed your uncle and struck me.

Kit. Did you come here to tell me that?

Laf. To tell you that it fired my soul like the spur maddens the steed—that I'm having a grand four-horse act of Equitation, to manage the tumultuous feelings your glance inspired. How do you like the comparison, eh?

Kit. I don't like the comparison, and don't like you! But I rather think, in your grand act of horsemanship, you must have met with an accident—come down on your head!

Laf. Bravo! If you can jump like that, you'll soon catch my meaning. [*Advancing.*]

Kit. [*Rising.*] I do not understand you, sir.

Laf. [*Trying to seize her hand.*] You charming little creature.

5

Kit. [*Retreating, followed by him.*] Leave me this instant. [*Crosses.*]

HERBERT *re-enters.*

Herbert. Stop, sir! What are you doing?

Laf. [*Aside.*] He's only half the size of the jackass slinger. [*Crosses to* R., *aloud.*] Who are you—and what are you?

Herb. My name is Rumbrent—I am a painter.

Laf. Painter—house or sign? He, he!

Herb. I shall be glad to paint a sign with your name and business on it. You are a coward and a ruffian!

Laf. [*Aside.*] No—he couldn't swing a jackass! [*Aloud and gives his card.*] There is my address—call on me when you like, and I'll give you the biggest job you ever had on your hands. [*Aside.*] He's no cannon ball tosser! I'm not afraid of him. [*Exits without his hat, after a profound bow to Kit.*]

Kit. [*Runs to Herb.*] There will be trouble! Do not bother with him! [*Getting* L.]

Herb. Don't be alarmed. We don't fight such fools in this country—we flog them, and if we did—I could die for you!

SPINKLE *re-enters, joyfully.*

Spinkle. They are going! They are going at last!

MRS. PORTLEY *enters, looking behind.*

Mrs. Portley. Do look! It's a regular procession!

Guests and servants enter. The windows and doors are filled with heads. ROSIE *enters on pony and* HERCULES *on donkey,* R. 2 E.

Hercules. We're off!

LAFAYETTE *re-enters,* L. U. E.

Lafayette. I forgot my hat.

Kit. [*Runs to Sp.*] My dear uncle!

Laf. He's her uncle!

Rosie. Good-bye, uncle!

Luf. She's his uncle! [*Turns in amazement—then perceives his hat. Takes it up and discovers the crown decorated by the colors from the palette.*] Heavens! [*Sits on palette.*] Good gracious! [*Rises with his coat decorated the same as his hat.*]

CURTAIN.

ACT IV.

SCENE.—*Same as Act First. Table laid for breakfast.*

SPINKLE *discovered at the window.*

Spinkle. How obedient she is! The shades are down.

JOHN *enters, with card,* C.

John. Mr. Spinkle.
Sp. Well?
John. A party just brought this card, sir.
Sp. [*Eagerly, after taking it.*] All right. You can go.

JOHN *exits after showing in* UNCLE MAJOR, *who enters, hat and umbrella in hand.*

Uncle. There you are.
Sp. [*Runs to him.*] It's all right. [*Showing him card.*] That's my policy of insurance for a quiet life.
Unc. [*Looks at it with glasses.*] Your own card?
Sp. It's the signal that the Wild Rose of Yucatan has gone. [*Crosses to* R.]
Unc. I congratulate you. So it won't be necessary for me to do anything in the business. I'm heartily glad of it. [*Turns card over.*] What's this on the back?
Sp. On the back?
Unc. Appears to be writing.
Sp. [*Takes it eagerly and reads.*] "She won't go. She has just received a billet-doux that upsets us. Will call on you as soon as I get particulars. Hercules." [*Crosses to* L.]

Unc. [R. C.] She's not gone! Then *I* am! [*Puts on hat and makes a start.*]

Sp. [*Catches him by coat-tail,* L. C.] Don't desert me!

Unc. There will be an explosion, sure! Your mother-in-law hasn't taken her departure yet, has she?

Sp. No—but I've ordered a gang of painters in the house. She can't bear the smell of paint, and is sure to retreat. Do stay!

Unc. She'll be in a terrible temper, then. I'd think I'd better be off. [*Another start.*]

Sp. [*Same play.*] Do me only one favor. Go and see my niece—the one across the way—invent anything to keep her away for this day at least. I'm sitting on a powder barrel.

Unc. I don't mind doing that. Not for your sake—you good-for-nothing rascal—but for her's—poor little girl! You deserve all you get. [*Exits,* C. L.]

Sp. We are back again in the old hole. It's fearful. What a lesson. If ever I experiment in the Arabian Nights again—

JOHN *enters, and puts letter on table,* L.

Sp. Has Mrs. Spinkle got home yet, John?

John. Yes, sir—but she's going out again.

LOUISE *enters,* R. U. D., *in calling-dress, but without hat or wraps.*

Sp. [*Arm round her neck.*] How lovely you look in that dress! Absolutely brilliant! Gorgeous!

Lou. [R. C.] You don't know how pleasant all your compliments sound. It's a treat to hear them, again—you flattering goose!

Sp. [L. C.] If you knew how famished I've been for somebody to talk to all the weeks we've been separated.

Lou. [R.] But you had mamma, darling!

Sp. Yes, darling, but I could not press her hand every moment, as I do yours.

Lou. I'm sure she'd have liked it, dearest.

Sp. Then I could not kiss her a hundred times a day, as I do you. [LOU. *sees John, and by a look calls Sp.'s attention to him.*] You may go, John. [JOHN *exits,* C.] And you are so cheerful, while mamma is occasionally—occasionally, you know—a little peevish, and that's so contagious—I caught the infection myself.

Lou. It's all over, now. Mamma meant well, and I'm sure paid you every attention.

Sp. Sometimes too much. She watched me like a cat. [*Stage,* L.]

Lou. Watched you?

Sp. [*Returning.*] I mean—watched everything I put in my mouth.

Lou. Why, she says you never took your meals at home!

Sp. Eh—exactly—that was the reason I didn't.

Lou. [*Half severely.*] And she says you were always on the go, and came home very late at night.

Sp. I really wish she had something more to tell! Why old women will meddle in other people's business I can't see! [*Crosses to* R.]

Lou. [*Reproachfully.*] Dearest!

Sp. It's positively malignant in her to embitter you against your husband the moment you step into the house. [*Crosses to* R.]

Lou. Embitter me against you! She will never succeed in doing that.

MRS. WEEBLES *enters,* R. U. D., *down* L., *holding handkerchief to her nose.*

Mrs. Weebles. I'd like to know who sent the painters up to my room?

Sp. [*Crosses to* L. C., *simulating wrath.*] The painters! Did the rascals come to-day?

Mrs. W. John says you sent for them.

Sp. [C.] I told them expressly to come when you had gone, and now I think of it, you said yourself you were going to-day.

Mrs. W. [*Crosses to* R.] Well, never mind. I've sent them about their business. [*Crosses. Sits* R *of table.* LOU. *sits* C. *and* SP. L.] Ah me! It's a long time since we had a comfortable meal together.

Sp. [L., *aside.*] Yes, it is, indeed! [*Aloud.*] That was because Louise was away.

Mrs. W. [R.] You can depend upon it, my children, true, real comfort, is only found with three in a family.

Sp. Three?

Mrs. W. Controversies can never arise—if a dispute occurs the majority decides.

Lou. [C.] I never thought of that. Mamma is quite right, isn't she, dear?

Sp. Well, the question immediately occurs, which is better: two women and one man in the house, or two men and one woman? [*With mouth full.*]

Lou. Yes, dear, but the question can't arise since we have mamma!

Sp. But she's going away.

Lou. But if you press her to stay, she will, won't you, mamma? [*About to take sugar—has the sugar-bowl in her* L. *hand—*SP.

shakes her hand and makes the sugar fly, and hastily puts every piece of sugar in his cup.] What do you want?

Sp. Eh? oh! The eggs. Hand me the eggs, please!

Lou. Here they are. [*Hands them.*]

Sp. [*To Mrs. W.*] I'm sure *we* lived in peace when we two were alone together, *we* never quarrelled.

Mrs. W. We couldn't. You hardly spoke to me.

Sp. Now that sounds like a complaint. Did I neglect you?

Mrs. W. Perhaps not—but there was your niece.

Sp. What about my niece?

Mrs. W. Letting her live away by herself.

Sp. We didn't have a room to offer her. You had the best one yourself.

Lou. [*Consoling her.*] Mamma, dear—

Sp. I give you my word, that the instant you go, I'll have her in.

Mrs. W. [*Moving chair away.*] Am I to understand, Mr. Spinkle, that this is a hint for me to go?

Lou. Why, mamma! It was only a little while ago he proposed that we should ask you to stay. [Sp. *pulls her dress.*] What do you want, dear?

Sp. Oh! The salt, please. [*Rises up,* c. l.]

Mrs. W. [*Rising.*] That's the way it was all the time you were gone.

Sp. [*Crosses and looks at watch.*] You were going out again, Louise?

Lou. [c., *rising.*] If my little niece comes, be sure and keep her till I come back, mamma.

Sp. [l.] She won't come. She's gone in the country.

Lou. [c.] In the country?

Sp. One of her shipboard acquaintances has invited her. I told her she ought to go.

Mrs. W. [r.] She might have called and said good-bye to me. I wrote to her to come. [*Aside.*] I wonder if Lafayette knows of this?

Lou. At all events, if she comes, keep her. [*Exits,* r.]

Mrs. W. [*To Sp.*] So you send your niece away, do you? You don't approve of her evident attachment to me. It is very kind of you, Mr. Spinkle.

Sp. I didn't send her away. They came for her.

Mrs. W. [*Anxiously.*] Are there any young men in the family she has gone to visit?

Sp. 'Pon my word, I don't know.

Mrs. W. It is criminally careless in you to let her run about the country in this way. Suppose she should fall in love?

Sp. I don't know. Let her please herself. It must come sooner or later.

Mrs. W. [*Anxiously.*] If some designing fortune hunter should snap her up!

Sp. Let him snap.

Mrs. W. You are a pretty one to be entrusted with the care of a young girl.

Sp. [*Majestically.*] I know nothing about young girls. I wish to know nothing about them. Excuse me—I'll go and order the carriage. [*Exits,* C. JOHN *removes the things.*]

Mrs. W. [*Alone.*] Hypocrite! He has detected Lafayette's attentions, and, to spite me, he has sent her out of the way. But I'll thwart him—I will.

LAFAYETTE *enters,* C. L.

Lafayette. Well, auntie! Have you spoken to Spinkle? Will he object?

Mrs. W. I can't speak to that man. You will have to approach him on the subject yourself. But I have my suspicions about his probable course. He has sent her away, and she may slip off completely.

Laf. [R.] With her money! And I bought her a perfectly stunning bouquet.

Mrs. W. Did you come to anything like a final understanding with her?

Laf. I came pretty near it; I got on my knees, you know.

Mrs. W. But what did she say?

Laf. She laughed right out.

Mrs. W. That is far from being decisive.

Laf. [*Winks.*] I gave her a kiss.

Mrs. W. You did? Did she cry?

Laf. No—she giggled. I think she was pleased.

Mrs. W. At all events, you are getting on.

Laf. [*Dubiously.*] Yes—I guess so—but she's awful skittish.

Mrs. W. [L.] And now about that creature over the way—did you have an interview?

Laf. No, I couldn't. Another acrobat turned up just as I was about to gain her confidence. A very low fellow. One of the persons I could not possibly converse with. His language was frightful.

Mrs. W. Then you discovered nothing?

Laf. Oh, I'm sure Spinkle is up to villainy there! He's passing her off on the landlady as his niece! I heard her address him—I'd learned more, but I met with an accident, and had to go home and change my clothes.

Mrs. W. That's quite enough! Passes her off as his niece! A female circus-rider! What is the world coming to? [*Crosses to* R., *with meaning.*] But say nothing! He's in our power—and we will bend him to our purpose—she is yours. [*Exits,* C. *to* R.]

Laf. If I hadn't sat on that paint, I could have clutched the fortune! She was going out to ride—I could have had a splendid *tete-a-tete* in the park—

SPINKLE *enters,* C. L., *quickly, but seeing Laf., attempts to go back, but* LAF. *sees him.*

Laf. Oh, cousin!

Spinkle. [L., *aside.*] I wonder how much the idiot saw across the way. [*Aloud.*] I'm in a great hurry. [*Going.*]

Laf. Only one word, please. I'm in a very peculiar position —I want to ask you—

Sp. [*Aside.*] Blackmail! The villain must be silenced! [*Aloud, taking out pocketbook.*] How much?

Laf. It's not that—I'm very much obliged—all I want is that I want to get married.

Sp. With all my heart! Good-bye. [*Going.*]

Laf. But I must talk to you about it further. You see, I have found a young lady who is very good looking—very amiable—very intelligent and very rich.

Sp. [R.] Young, rich and intelligent, eh? Well, if she's intelligent, you'd better give it up—it's no go. Lafayette, you've no chance.

Laf. She loves me—but we require the consent of her relatives—one especially.

Sp. Do you wish me to go and see him?

Laf. Oh, no; let me tell you how it is.

Sp. I havn't time for a long story. I know the facts already —she is young, amiable, intelligent and rich. You love each other. Now, what do you want?

Laf. [*Dropping on his knees.*] Your blessing on our union.

Sp. With pleasure! Bless you! [*Hastily waves his hands over him and turns away, up* L.]

Laf. Really and truly?

Sp. My son—you are not well! Are you off your chump? You're out of your senses.

Laf. A little.

Sp. A little! That's all there was.

Laf. Let me hug you! [*Embraces him.*]

Sp. [*Wriggling away.*] Pray, who is the lady?

Laf. You know.

Sp. I?

Laf. I met her here.

Sp. You met her here?

Laf. In this very house. Who should it be but your charming niece!

Sp. [*Thunderstruck.*] My niece! [*Aside.*] Heavens! which one? [*Crosses to* R.]

Laf. Your mother-in-law managed it for me.

Sp. My mother-in-law! [*Aside.*] Then it's Rosie! [*Aloud.*] My dear cousin, my answer will be short and to the point. It's impossible.

Laf. Impossible?

Sp. Simply impossible. Don't speak. I won't hear a word. The thing is out of the question.

Laf. But Spinkle—my dear Spinkle!

Sp. Look at the matter coolly. My brother sends his daughter over here to await his arrival, and you think I would dispose of her in this manner—to the first comer? No, sir, not even if you were a fit object for her regard.

Laf. [*Dismayed.*] Not even if I were a fit object!

Sp. Although you are not a fit object, you can see the force of my reasons.

MRS. WEEBLES *enters,* C.

Laf. I'll telegraph to her father.

Sp. You'll do nothing of the kind. It's impossible.

Mrs. Weebles. [*Violently, down* C.] Impossible, Mr. Spinkle, and why impossible, if you please?

Sp. [R., *aside.*] The old lady! Now for a scene.

Mrs. W. [C., *wheedling.*] My dear son-in-law, let us reason the thing over.

Laf. [L.] Yes, let aunt reason the thing over with you.

Sp. [*Crosses to* C.] I say "no" and there's an end of it.

Mrs. W. [*In a rage.*] It's mere spite! You refuse because I wish it.

Sp. Put it on any ground you please. [*To Laf.*] I say "no!" [*To Mrs. W.*] Emphatically—No!! N-O! [*Goes up, turns near door.*] No!!! [*Exits,* R. D.]

Laf. You hear him?

Mrs. W. [R.] I'll tame him. I'll teach him to raise his voice and N-O me.

Laf. Well, I don't give up the ship. There's one way left. I'll elope with her.

Mrs. W. It would serve him right. I should not blame her. Will she go? [*Confidentially.*] Meanwhile, I'll take my precious son-in-law in hand. You'll see him beg for mercy. But you must bring her here before you go—my consent and advice will turn the scales if she is inclined to hesitate.

Laf. I'll bring her here. [*Exits, c. l.*]

SPINKLE *re-enters*, R. U. D.

Spinkle. Now, that he's gone, we can talk this matter over seriously. You are a woman of sense. It would be the greatest favor to me if you would get this ridiculous idea out of his head.

Mrs. W. [L.] Oh, you consent to talk it over with me, do you? [*Sits L. of c. table.*]

Sp. [*Sits.*] I could not speak before Lafayette. But let me assure you in the beginning that my resolution is unalterable.

Mrs. W. Are you quite sure of that?

Sp. Quite! And I am prepared to say that you cannot remain in my house if you encourage him in his folly.

Mrs. W. [*Mockingly.*] Really! Well, before you commit yourself to that resolution, permit me to tell you a little story.

Sp. A little story?

Mrs. W. A story with a moral. It is entitled, "The Impertinent Husband, or the Beautiful Circus Rider." [SP. *arises, frightened, his eye fixed on her.*] Aha! it interests you, don't it?

Sp. Not very much! [*Sits.*] I can't see why it should.

Mrs. W. [*Taps his arm with her fan.*] I know all about it, my dear son-in-law.

Sp. [*Aside.*] Is it possible! [*Aloud.*] All about what?

Mrs. W. She has confessed everything.

Sp. [*Leans back in his chair with a gasp, then recovers himself.*] Then, you know how perfectly innocent I am. [MRS. W. *laughs.*] Now, don't laugh. It was an accident—a foolish whim.

Mrs. W. [*Jeeringly.*] Of course! Of course!

Sp. It was all along of Haroun al Raschid, you know. She told you about Haroun al Raschid?

Mrs. W. [*Aside.*] Haroun al Raschid? What does he mean? [*Aloud.*] Certainly, she told me everything.

Sp. And you know that the cannon ball man has come to take her off my hands.

Mrs. W. Of course! [*Aside.*] A pretty set he's got in with.

Sp. [*Moves his chair close to hers.*] And now, as you know everything, let us talk openly. What do you intend to do?

Mrs. W. What a sensible woman would do under the circumstances. I intend to help you.

Sp. [*Overjoyed.*] You do, really?

Mrs. W. Although you don't deserve it.

Sp. [*Affectionately.*] How I have misunderstood you, my dear mamma.

Mrs. W. And now—if I assist you—you must assist Lafayette.

Sp. Lafayette! How much does he know about all this?

Mrs. W. He knows everything.

Sp. [*Astonished.*] He does! Well, then—I don't understand how he can—

LOUISE *enters in street dress,* R. U. E.

Mrs. W. —'Sh! Louise is here! [*They rise.*]

Louise. [*In archway,* C.] Are you ready, dear?

Sp. Yes, my love! [*Crosses to* C., *aside to Mrs. W.*] I'll be back as soon as I can.

Mrs. W. [R., *same to him.*] But she may be gone before you get back.

Sp. [*Aside.*] So much the better! [*Aloud to Lou.*] I'm coming. Good-bye, mamma.

Lou. [*Aside to Sp., taking his arm.*] That's right. [*To Mrs. W.*] Good-bye, dear mamma.

Sp. Yes—good-bye, *dear* mamma! [*Exeunt,* C.]

Mrs. W. He can't escape! How I twisted him round my finger, when I began my little story. He didn't wait to hear it out, but surrendered at once! [*Goes to window.*] They are gone! [*Aside.*] I'd give something to know who Haroun al Raschid is, though. I must find that out. [L.]

John. [*Outside.*] But I tell you he's just gone out.

Herbert. [*Outside.*] Very well. If Mr. Spinkle is not at home, anybody will do. I've got a message to deliver.

Mrs. W. [*Pausing.*] Who is that?

JOHN *ushers in* HERBERT.

John. Here's Mr. Spinkle's mother.

Herbert. [*Entrance,* C. L.] I must entreat your pardon, madam, but the singular circumstances in which I am placed, will excuse my intrusion.

Mrs. W. What do you wish, sir?

Herb. [R.] I have come to this house to demand an explanation, and to clear up a mystery.

Mrs. W. [L.] You seem to be greatly excited, sir.

Herb. I confess it, madam. And the cause of it is the unwarrantable conduct of Mr. Spinkle to a young lady in the opposite house, whom Mr. Spinkle calls his niece.

Mrs. W. [L., *aside.*] The creature! This must be the cannon-ball man, who is to take her off his hands! [*Aloud and stiffly.*] The matter does not concern me in the least, sir.

Herb. I was prepared for the evasion. But as the young lady claims to be under Mr. Spinkle's protection—

Mrs. W. Don't, I beg of you—I can't permit—

Herb. I will be extremely brief. I love the young lady, and I firmly believe, as far as judgment can assure it, that my love is returned.

Mrs. W. Very well, sir. I have no objection to that.

Herb. But what will Mr. Spinkle say to this avowal?

Mrs. W. I answer for him! He'll be delighted.

Herb. Then I have only to announce that I take her back to her own home to-morrow.

Mrs. W. You have my congratulations. Do you wish Mr. Spinkle to pay your fares?

Herb. We are greatly obliged, but will not trouble him.

Mrs. W. Allow me to say, on our part, that we are delighted to get rid of the young lady in that or any other manner. [*Crosses to* R.]

Herb. You are excessively kind.

Mrs. W. You surely don't expect me to take any interest in that kind of a niece, I hope?

Herb. Oh, no. She is poor and would have been a burden to you. Nevertheless, I could not take the step I propose, without her uncle's consent.

Mrs. W. Don't be uneasy. Do what you please. Go, stay, love, marry—we will offer no objections.

Herb. Thanks, madam! Be assured we shall never trouble you again. [*Exits,* C.]

Mrs. W. For a circus performer his manners are really very good. [*Looks at clock.*] Kate must soon be here. The dear child shall have my locket to take with her, as a proof of my interest and affection. [*Exits,* R. U. D.]

JOHN *enters, followed by* HERCULES, *who is quite hilarious,* C. L.

Hercules. [R.] I tell you, my fine fellow, I am a particular friend of Mr. Spinkle.

John. That may all be so, sir. But I tell you he's not in at present.

Her. What of that? He's bound to come back some time! What time will he be back? [*Slapping him on the back.*]

John. He may be in very soon. There's no telling.

Her. [*Crosses to* R.] Then we'll wait for him. Don't ask me to take a seat, because I was just about to do it. [*Sits on sofa.*] And you needn't bring any refreshments until your master comes in. He'll order up the suitable. Now go, John, clean up the knives and forks. I won't detain you any longer.

John. [*Aside.*] I don't like to leave him alone. I guess I'd better get the mother-in-law out—she'll know how to dispose of him. [*Crosses to and exits,* R. U. D.]

Her. My friend Spinkle don't lodge badly. Everything of the best. If it was my house, though, I'd have pictures of the best horses hung round the room, and a couple of dumb bells on the centre table. And as for these lazy flunkeys, I'd have 'em up twice a day and trot 'em round the ring. [*Cracks whip and gets back to sofa.*]

JOHN *re-enters,* R. U. D., *crosses.*

John. She's a coming. [*Exits,* C. L.]

MRS. WEEBLES *enters,* R. U. D.

Mrs. Weebles. A strange man in the parlor?

Her. [*Yawning and stretching.*] I suppose there's time for a little nap! [*Curls up on sofa, with his back to Mrs. W.*]

Mrs. W. Do you wish to see Mr. Spinkle, sir?

Her. [*Jumping up.*] Mr. Spinkle! Where is the old boy?

Mrs. W. The old boy!

Her. You bet your life he's on a cruise somewhere. He's got nothing to do but enjoy himself.

Mrs. W. May I ask with whom I have the honor of speaking?

Her. Honors are easy, I guess, old lady. I suppose you're the housekeeper. I'm one of the heavy-weights—under man in the pyramid—ground and lofty tumbling, eh?

Mrs. W. [L., *aside.*] Another acrobat! My son-in-law is certainly going to set up a circus.

Her. This sort of a rig don't set off a fellow. You ought to see me in tights. If you're a judge of muscle, there's your chance. [*Nudging her.*]

Mrs. W. But what do you want in my son-in-law's house?

Her. [*Crosses to* L.] Your son-in-law! [*Whistles.*] Then I guess I made a pretty considerable mistake! I apologize. This performance will not be repeated by request. [*Bows.*]

Mrs. W. Your business?

Her. My business! Ah! that's the point. First—let me ask one question. Are you on good terms with your son-in-law?

Mrs. W. Of course. He has no secrets from me.

Her. [*Nudging her.*] Very good. Then as you know all about this affair, of course—I merely came to say that the fat's in the fire—she won't go.

Mrs. W. She won't go? The—the lady circus performer?

Her. There's a chap hanging round who wants to marry her. Now you know that when a woman gets *that* in her head, you can't do anything with her. You've been there. *You* know.

Mrs. W. [R] Sir! Come to the case in point.

Her. The point's just here. My governor expects me to bring her to the circus to-morrow. He's got to have her. If I go back without her, he'll just pull my head off. Yes he will.

Mrs. W. Then let me inform you that the young man *is* going to marry her. He was here just now.

Her. He was? You saw him?

Mrs. W. He must belong to a rival establishment—his business is connected with cannon balls—if you understand what that is?

Her. You don't tell me! Going to take her to another establishment, is he?

Mrs. W. You had better consult him yourself.

Her. [*Rolls up his cuffs.*] I'll consult him. Look here! There's a cannon ball I'll give him to toss. There's a fifty-six pounder for him to lift off his nose. Much obliged to you. I'll ring up on as pretty a show as you ever see when I catch him. [*Going up,* L.]

Mrs. W. One moment, please.

Her. [*At door, turns.*] I'm on time.

Mrs. W. Do you know anything about Haroun al Raschid?

Her. [L.] Haroun al Raschid?

Mrs. W. I'm exceedingly anxious to know all about him.

Her. Haroun-al-Raschid! Why he's the best trick horse of our circus; goes up a step-ladder like a Christian, fires off a pistol with his teeth, and turns a hand-organ with his off left foot. [*Returns and gives her tickets.*] Here's a couple of comps for the show next month. You'll see the entire animal if you come. Good day, ma'am. No thanks. Don't mention it. [*Off* C., *quickly.* MUSIC.]

Mrs. W. What a fearful class of people! But what in the name of common sense had the horse to do with my son-in-law's infatuation for this creature? He said it was all on account of Haroun al Raschid. [*Crosses to* L.] More mystery. [*Goes to window.*] Here they are! Lafayette and the dear child, in a cab. He has brought her at last—it was time. Now I can make them happy.

LAFAYETTE *and* ROSIE *enter*, C. R.

Lafayette. Here we are, aunty!

Mrs. W. [L., *embraces Ros.*] My sweet girl! [*Crosses to* C., *to Laf.*] So you are happy, you foolish fellow?

Laf. [R.] I feel as if I was standing on my head.

Rosie. I don't know what's the matter with him.

Mrs. W. It is love, my precious. All your doing—enchantress. [MUSIC *stops.*]

Ros. [*Draws Mrs. W. aside, and quietly.*] Did you know he wants to marry me?

Mrs. W. The impetuous boy.

Ros. [*Same.*] And he wants me to elope with him.

Mrs. W. Just like him. You'll have to do it. There never was any resisting him. [*Crosses to* C.]

Ros. [L.] Will you answer me one question, please? [*To* LAF., *who draws near.*] No, no; you must not listen.

Mrs. W. [L.] Go away, you naughty fellow! [LAF. *goes up*, R.] What is it, my child?

Ros. [C.] When people wish to get married, I suppose they must have something to live upon. How much has *he* got?

Mrs. W. My dear child, what he possesses is of minor importance. *You* will have enough for both.

Ros. Oh—so we can live on *my* fortune?

Mrs. W. [*Crosses to* C., *patting her on cheek.*] Yes, you practical little thing.

Ros. Ya'as. I *am* a practical little thing—and I like to have a practical little husband. Has Lafayette considered the circumstances you mention?

Mrs. W. Oh, fully. [*Goes to Laf.*]

Ros. [L., *aside.*] So that's the romance of it, is it?

Laf. [C., *goes to Ros.*] The brightest future opens before us. The sky is all sunshine. We will live in air.

Ros. [*Aside.*] Yes, and on it.

Laf. Let us wing our flight to the empyrean of happiness.

Ros. [*Looks at him.*] Houp-la!

Mrs. W. [*Contemplating them.*] You were created for each other. [MUSIC.]

Ros. [*Aside.*] How happy a girl must be when all this is real! Poor Rosie! [*Dashes away a tear.*] Time to be off! [*Gaily, crosses to* C.]

Mrs. W. [*Puts locket and chain over Ros.'s neck.*] Keep this for my sake.

Ros. You have been very kind to me. I'm grateful. [*Lays her hand on Mrs. W.'s arm.*] And you shall not regret it. [*With meaning.*]

SPINKLE *enters and looks at the group, astonished.* ROS. *sees him and goes to him.*

Ros. Good-bye. [LAF. *crosses to Mrs. W.*]

Spinkle. [*As he takes Ros.'s hand, says in a low tone to her.*] This time I hope for good.

Ros. [*Same to him.*] Most generous Haroun al Raschid, the stay has come to an end at last. Don't be afraid. I'll return him [*Indicating Laf.*] safe and sound.

Mrs. W. Don't keep them! They must go!

Laf. Come, my dear! Good-bye, cousin! [*To Spink.*] We are off!

Sp. [R., *near arch, shaking hands with him.*] Take my advice. Get an excursion ticket—there and back. [Ros. *and* LAF. *exit, off* C.]

Mrs. W. Bless them!

Sp. [R., *coming down.*] You won't tell Louise anything of what you know?

Mrs. W. Not for the present.

Sp. [*Alarmed.*] The present?

Mrs. W. [R.] Not till the dear children come back from their honeymoon.

Sp. Their honeymoon!

Mrs. W. [*Triumphantly.*] We have taken you by surprise. You have just assisted at their elopement. [*Crosses to* L.]

Sp. [*Excited.*] Elopement? Do you know what you have done?

Mrs. W. Done! Yes—done you! [*Crosses to* R., *up.*] Ha, ha, ha, Mr. Spinkle! Outwitted by your stupid old mother-in-law! ha, ha, ha! [*Exits,* R. U. D.]

Sp. [*His back against table.*] When the truth comes out—I don't want to see her. That laugh in passing around to the other side of her mouth will certainly wrench her.

UNCLE *enters,* C., *quickly, and puts down hat. Down* R.

Uncle. I say, Spinkle, did you know she was going away?

Sp. Going? She has gone.

Unc. [*Wipes forehead.*] No—not yet.

Sp. [*Alarmed.*] Not gone yet!

Unc. I tried my best to keep her.

Sp. [*Angrily.*] Why, what the devil—what in the name of madness induced you to do that?

Unc. I mean your niece across the way.

Sp Eh! Oh, yes. I am so confused I forgot my niece.

But you say *she* is going. Everybody is going except my mother-
in-law! [*To Unc.*] Going where?

Unc. Home! The poor thing was ready to cry.

Sp. [*Crosses to* R.] I'd like to cry, myself—I feel as if I
were about to be hanged. Fancy what has happened! Lafayette has eloped with the circus girl!

Unc. The Arabian Nights girl—the bare-back rider? Well
—all I can say is—it's a nice mess you've got into.

Sp. When the truth comes out, I'm ruined! Help me, uncle!
Think—invent—

Unc. When the truth comes out! Bring it out yourself—
draw the string! Confess!

Sp. To Mrs. Weebles?

Unc. To your wife.

Sp. [*Looks mournfully at him.*] You advise that?

Unc. I do.

Sp. The clouds are gathering.

Unc. The truth will scatter them, my boy—and after the
storm—a bright morning.

Sp. And the thunder and lightning will be furnished by my
mother-in-law. [*Exits,* R. U. D.]

LOUISE *enters,* C. L., *followed by* SUSAN, *who helps to remove her
cloak and hat.*

Louise. Mr. Spinkle is home?

Susan. [L.] Yes, ma'am. Please, m'm, there's a young lady
down stairs, who's been waiting for you. [MUSIC.]

Lou. [R.] A young lady? Ask her to come up.

KITTY *appears at door.*

Kitty. I took the liberty—[SUSAN *exits,* L.]

Lou. Why, my dear Kate, when did you get back?

Kit. I have not been away!

Lou. Why, my husband said you had gone to visit some
friends!

Kit. Don't be angry with me, aunt, but uncle has been acting
so strangely.

Lou. Strangely?

Kit. Yes. I have made up my mind to go back to papa. If
it had not been for Herbert—

Lou. Herbert? Who is Herbert?

Kit. I didn't tell you. He is in love with me.

6

Lou. [*Reproach, alarm.*] Heavens! what have you been doing?

Kit. [L.] We have been consulting as to the best course to take under the circumstances.

SPINKLE *enters quickly, followed by* UNCLE.

Spinkle. My dear— [*Stops on seeing Kit.*]

Uncle. [R.] Now's your time!—confess everything!

Lou. [L. C., *goes to Sp.*] My dear, I'm so glad you've come. This poor child has taken a most important step.

Sp. [*Drawing her away.*] Yes—and I'm going to take a most important step.

Lou. [C.] But she acknowledges—

Sp. I am going to acknowledge—I must see you alone. [UNC. *goes up stage.*]

Lou. But she—

Sp. It's about her—and—others I wish to speak. If you don't come now it'll all fizz out! [*Feeling his throat.*] I've got the cork out and there's not a moment to lose! [*Exit,* R. U. D., *with Lou.*]

Kit. [*Aside.*] More mystery! I'm getting frightened again. [*Sits,* L. C., *table.*]

Unc. [L.] Sit down! Don't be frightened! It'll be all right within five minutes. I'll go and bring somebody else! [*Nods, winks, smiles and exits,* C. L.]

MRS. WEEBLES *enters,* R. U. D., *stops on seeing Kit.*

Mrs. Weebles. That circus creature here! Whom are you waiting for? [*Tartly.*]

Kit. [L., *rises.*] For Mr. Spinkle.

Mrs. W. [*Sternly.*] I thought you were gone—long ago.

Kit. [*Interested.*] Did you know I had resolved to go back?

Mrs. W. Yes—and I am particularly desirous of knowing why you have changed your mind!

Kit. I have not changed my mind. I thought it my duty to come here and say good-bye.

Mrs. W. Your sense of duty, young woman, seems a little exaggerated. Come! If there is anything more you want, tell me, you needn't see anybody else. In fact, I advise you not to!

Kit. [*Rises proudly.*] I am not afraid to see anybody] Everybody knows who I am. I am not ashamed. [*Crosses* R. C.]

Mrs W. [*Aside.*] The brazen thing!

Kit. Aunt herself told me to wait here.

Mrs. W. Aunt? What aunt?

Kit. It seems you don't know me. I am Mr. Spinkle's niece from France.

Mrs. W. You bold, audacious creature! Ain't you afraid the floor will open and swallow you up?

UNCLE *and* HERBERT *enter, c.*

Uncle. There she is.

Herbert. [R. C., *goes to Kit.*] Why do you remain with these people, love?

Mrs. W. She brings her acrobats under our very noses!

Kit. [R.] Things are worse and worse! I have just been called a bold, audacious creature. Somebody's crazy here, and I know it's not me.

LOUISE *enters, R. U. E., laughing, and pulling in* SPINKLE.

Louise. It's a splendid story! [*Runs to Kit., and seizes both her hands.*] My poor Kate, what must you have suffered!

Mrs. W. Louise, do you know in what relation that person stands to your husband?

Lou. Yes, mamma. She's his niece.

Mrs. W. His niece?

Spinkle. [C., *going to Mrs. W.*] Of course, didn't you know that? You said you knew everything?

Mrs. W. [*In alarm.*] Tell me, then!—for goodness sake! How many nieces have you got?

Sp. Only one—this one.

Mrs. W. And the circus rider? Where is she?

Sp. Eloped with Lafayette! [*Goes to Lou., Kit. and Herb.* MRS. W. *screams and faints.* UNC. *supports her to a chair, and begins to slap her hands.*]

Lou. Poor mamma! [*About to go to her.*]

Sp. [*Restraining her.*] Wait a moment. She'll brace up in a minute. I feel it coming. [*To Herb.*] I have heard all about it. For the present you shall be a welcome guest in my house, until my brother arrives! He will give you his answer.

Mrs. W. [*Suddenly reviving.*] Where is he? [*Jumps up.*]

Sp. She wants me.

Mrs. W. [*Approaching him.*] You have deceived me! entrapped us! Give me back that poor deluded young man!

Sp. I regret to say I cannot.

ROSIE *appears at door.*

Rosie. But I can!

Mrs. W. You?

Ros. You recollect—I told you you were kind to me—and you should not regret it. Here is your locket—it was not meant for *me.* And here is your nephew—he was not exactly intended for me, either.

LAFAYETTE *enters, with handkerchief tied over his eye and limping.*

Lafayette. Oh, auntie! we've had a devil of a time! [L. *of Ros.*]

Ros. I promised to bring him back safe and sound—but—[*To Mrs. W.*] you told poor Hercules that he was a rival circus man trying to carry me off, and so, in his indignation—

Laf. He began to cannon ball me! First, he loaded me with abuse, and then fired me into the middle of the street.

Ros. But then he apologized when he discovered his mistake.

Laf. [*Producing tickets.*] Yes, and he gave me two complimentary tickets for the show. [*Crosses to* R.]

Ros. And brought you here himself!

HERCULES *appears sheepishly at back.*

Mrs. W. My poor Lafayette! We will go together.

Unc. [L.] No, you shall not. [MUSIC.]

Ros. And now I can go—and *this* time for good.

Lou. [*Goes to Ros.*] No, you shall not—at least not till we have had a chat together. I am the only person who has a right to complain—and I have nothing to complain of.

Sp. Angel!

Herb. A true woman!

Kit. The best in the world.

Mrs. W. Too good for this earth.

Hercules. [R. *of Mrs. W., feeling in his pocket, aside.*] And I gave away my last two comps for the great show to that duffer over there. [*Down* L.]

Ros. [*To Lou.*] And you don't think badly of poor little me! How is it possible?

Lou. Because your big blue eyes look me straight in the face—

Ros. Ah, no! it's because a good woman believes in goodness—and there's not one here—no, not one, I'm sure, that's honest himself or herself—but will believe in the innocence of our Haroun al Raschid—

Sp. And his own particular Arabian Nights.

CURTAIN.

AN

ARABIAN NIGHT

IN THE

NINETEENTH CENTURY.

A COMEDY IN FOUR ACTS, FROM THE GERMAN,
OF VON MOSER.

BY

AUGUSTIN DALY.

AS ACTED AT DALY'S THEATRE FOR THE FIRST TIME,
NOVEMBER 29TH, 1879.

NEW YORK:
PRINTED AS MANUSCRIPT ONLY, FOR THE AUTHOR.
1884.

www.ingramcontent.com/pod-product-compliance
Lightning Source LLC
Chambersburg PA
CBHW020048030726
47499CB00007B/2640